Welcome to the Secret W⟨...⟩

My family decided to take a vacation to Las Vegas—so here we are, in the middle of giant castles, ancient pyramids, and erupting volcanoes! We were having a great time—my dad using one of his formulas to win on the roulette wheel, and Annie, Ray, and I all seeing the sights. But then Annie's newfound friend stole her notebook—the one with all the information about me in it! I have to get it back right away, or my secret won't be a secret anymore! Let me explain. . . .

I'm Alex Mack. I was just another average kid until my first day of junior high.

One minute I'm walking home from school—the next there's a *crash!* A truck from the Paradise Valley Chemical plant overturns in front of me and I'm drenched in some weird chemical.

And since then—well, nothing's been the same. I can move objects with my mind, shoot electrical charges through my fingertips, and morph into a liquid shape . . . which is handy when I get in a tight spot!

My best friend, Ray, thinks it's cool—and my sister, Annie, thinks I'm a science project.

They're the only two people who know about my new powers. I can't let anyone else find out—not even my parents—because I know the chemical plant wants to find me and turn me into some experiment.

But you know something? I guess I'm not so average anymore!

The Secret World of Alex Mack

Available from MINSTREL Books

NICKELODEON®

the secret world of

ALEX MACK™

Lost in Vegas!

John Peel

A MINSTREL® BOOK

Published by POCKET BOOKS
New York   London   Toronto   Sydney   Tokyo   Singapore

This book is a work of fiction. Names, characters, places and incidents are products of the author's imagination or are used fictitiously. Any resemblance to actual events or locales or persons, living or dead, is entirely coincidental.

A MINSTREL PAPERBACK *Original*

 A Minstrel Book published by
POCKET BOOKS, a division of Simon & Schuster Inc.
1230 Avenue of the Americas, New York, NY 10020

Copyright   1998 by Viacom International Inc., and RHI Entertainment, Inc. All rights reserved. Based on the Nickelodeon series entitled "The Secret World of Alex Mack."

ISBN: 0-671-00710-6

First Minstrel Books printing January 1998

10 9 8 7 6 5 4 3 2 1

NICKELODEON, The Secret World of Alex Mack and all related titles, logos and characters are trademarks of Viacom International Inc.

A MINSTREL BOOK and colophon are registered trademarks of Simon & Schuster Inc.

Front cover photo by Pat Hill Studio

Printed in the U.S.A.

This is for Amanda Cestaro

Lost in Vegas!

CHAPTER 1

"So, Alex," Louis Driscoll asked, sliding up to her at the lunch table. "What are you going to be doing during the midterm break?"

Alex Mack sighed and placed her juice carton back on her tray. "Don't you get bored asking that same question every day, Louis, and getting the same answer?"

"Nope," Louis replied, grinning. "Only three days to go, and you're still doing nada, hey? Did I mention that my family's off to Seattle for five days?"

"Only about five hundred times," Nicole growled. "And if you don't stop, you're liable to spend the time in the hospital instead, because the rest of us will jump up and down on you."

Louis shook his head in mock sorrow. "Thus speaks the voice of jealousy. I know, you all wish you could be Louis Driscoll, too. Sadly, there's just one of me."

Raymond Alvarado raised his eyebrows. He liked Louis, but sometimes the other boy didn't realize he was going a bit too far. "There'll be one less of you if you don't stop tormenting everyone," he pointed out.

"There may be one less of him anyway," Robyn—the final member of the group at the lunch table—commented. "He'll be eating airline food, and that's even worse than cafeteria food. Plastic chicken in rubber sauce. Ugh."

Louis wasn't going to let her get to him. "Actually, I like airline food," he said cheerfully. "Personal service, and no need to bother with a drive-through."

Alex started to get up. "I'm going inside. I don't think there's enough room out here for all of us and Louis's ego."

"You're just jealous," Louis repeated smugly, as the others joined Alex on the retreat indoors.

"There are times," Nicole said, "when I'd just

love to push that smug face of his into a bowl of chocolate pudding."

That thought made Alex giggle. "Only times?" she asked.

"Yes." Nicole gave a smile. "Every time I see him."

"He's not all *that* bad," Ray said, feeling that he'd better stick up for his friend since it looked like no one else was going to.

"I know, Ray," Alex agreed. "He can be a lot of fun. But he'd be a lot more likable if he stopped rubbing in his family trip when he knows the rest of us are stuck here in Paradise Valley. As if we don't *all* wish we were going somewhere else for a few days. I mean, Paradise Valley is okay, but we all want to spread our wings and see more of the world."

"Not me," Robyn said firmly. "I get depressed enough at home. I don't need to go somewhere else and become more depressed."

Nicole shook her head. "Has it ever occurred to you that maybe you'd be *happier* somewhere else?"

"It's not very likely," Robyn pointed out.

Nicole decided that they needed to change the subject. "So, Alex," she asked as they seated themselves indoors to continue their lunch, "what's life like without Annie home?"

Alex considered the point before speaking. Her older sister, Annie, had just started college, leaving Alex alone with her parents for the first time since she was born. "There's a lot of good things," Alex replied. "I don't have to share my room now. Or the bathroom. And she's not always around offering me free advice that I don't want. So that's all great. On the other hand, I do kind of miss her. And she wouldn't let me oversleep the alarm." Alex had a habit of doing that, and had managed to get into trouble for arriving late twice so far this term.

There was another aspect of Annie's not being around that affected Alex a lot. Annie was one of only two people who knew Alex's secret— that she had been showered in a secret chemical called GC-161 as a result of a truck accident. The illegal chemical had been manufactured at Paradise Valley Chemical, the largest business in town, and its effects were unknown—to all but Alex, Annie, and Ray. Alex had developed strange powers that she had to hide from everyone, for the sake of safety. Annie had been checking on her powers and making sure that

4

Alex wasn't suffering any ill effects from the chemical bath. To do this, Annie had forced Alex to undergo a lot of testing that had strained her patience. But Alex knew that Annie had only performed those tests out of concern for her little sister. So it was something that Alex felt very ambivalent about. She'd hated being her sister's pet guinea pig, but at the same time she had loved her sister for caring so much about her.

But this was something that she had to keep hidden from Nicole and Robyn. The fewer people who knew her secret, the safer she was. Danielle Atron, the cold, money-hungry boss of Paradise Valley Chemical, had spent the last few years since the accident hunting for the GC-161 kid, and Alex knew that if Ms. Atron ever discovered that Alex was that child, then Alex's life would change drastically. She'd be locked up and subjected to experimentation.

Nicole nodded in sympathy. "A kind of yin and yang thing," she commented. "Good and bad, both at the same time."

"That's it," agreed Alex. "But I do miss her sometimes, even though we didn't always get along."

"That's the way life is," Robyn said mournfully. "When we get what we want—we discover it's not what we wanted after all."

"It *is* what I wanted," Alex contradicted her. "Most of the time, at any rate. It's just now and then I like being with her. And I can't be, because she's at college."

Alex couldn't help remembering the conversation later that evening at home. She had helped her mother prepare dinner, waiting for Alex's father to get home from the plant. Alex didn't mind helping out with the work, because it was pretty light, and she enjoyed helping her mother. But until recently, there had been three of them doing it, and Annie's absence was quite noticeable.

"Mom," she asked, as she laid out the silverware, "do you miss Annie?"

Her mother nodded. "Of course I do, Alex. It's such a major step when one of your children grows up and leaves home to go out into the world for herself." She smiled and patted Alex on the shoulder. "And you'll be following her soon enough."

Alex grimaced at the thought. "But I don't have a clue what I want to do with my life," she protested. "I don't even know if I want to go to college."

"Well, I'm sure you'll make your mind up soon," her mother answered. "And then our home will *really* start feeling empty." She sighed.

Alex realized that bringing up Annie had been a bad idea, so she said the only other thing that was on her mind to try to change the subject. "Louis and his family are going to Seattle over the break."

"That's nice." Her mother suddenly stopped and thought for a moment. "You know, Alex, that's not a bad idea."

"What isn't?" Alex had no clue what her mother meant.

"Going away for a few days," Mom replied, her eyes lighting up. "Annie will be off, and you and I are, too." Her mother was taking courses at a local college, which was also closed for a week. "And I know your father has a lot of vacation time accumulated." Her face became firm. "When he comes home, I'm going to suggest it to him."

Alex could hardly believe it—Mom was actually thinking about taking a vacation. A *family* vacation, and bringing Annie along on it, too. It would be really good to see her sister again for a few days. That was long enough for them both to enjoy each other's company again, and not long enough to get on one another's nerves. It sounded like a terrific idea! *If* Dad went for it. He could be a bit of a workaholic at times.

Mr. Mack struggled in the door about ten minutes later, looking exhausted. He fumbled his briefcase to the chair by the door, and his coat into the closet. Alex gave him a quick hug, and he winced.

"Thanks for the enthusiastic greeting, Alex," he said tiredly. "But I don't think it's going to help my back."

"Poor George," said Mrs. Mack. "Come and sit down, and we'll get your dinner. You look terrible. Did you have a bad day at the plant?" Like almost everyone else in town, Alex's father worked at Paradise Valley Chemical. In fact, he had been one of the team of scientists exploring the nature of GC-161. Now, however, he'd been transferred to another project, and he was working hard at coming up to speed with the research.

"One of those days when inspiration just won't come," Mr. Mack admitted with a deep sigh. "I'm working on this new mathematical projection formula that should help me to predict some of the nonlinear properties of my test subject, but I just can't make the final link in my mind. It's fascinating and frustrating, and I feel that if I could just rework the bipolar constant . . ." He broke off as he saw the expressions on the faces of Alex and her mother. "Oh, I'm sorry," he apologized. He helped himself to the mashed potatoes. "I'm just so used to talking things over with Annie. I keep forgetting that she isn't here. I know I can go on a bit too much about my work sometimes."

Alex's mother gave Alex a big smile. "Well, Alex had a terrific idea. Why not take a few days off and have a family vacation? And have Annie join us?" She leaned forward sympathetically and patted his hand. "I think it sounds like you need a few days off from the lab to get your mind back into gear again." She finished serving the food, and they all started to eat.

"Oh, no, I couldn't possibly take time off now," he replied automatically. Alex's hopes were dashed again, just as it had started looking like they might be having some fun after all. "I really have to get this formula working." Then he paused and frowned. "On the other hand, it *is* the only thing I have to do right now, and I *don't* have a clue as to how to get it right. And it *might* be a good idea to talk it over with Annie. Get everything straight in my mind . . ." Suddenly he beamed at them both. "Yes, I don't see why not. I'll just tell Ms. Atron tomorrow that I want a few days off to relax my mind. I've got plenty of time accumulated, and there's nobody else off right now. I'm sure it wouldn't be a problem."

"George, that's marvelous!" Mrs. Mack exclaimed. "It'll be wonderful for us to just spend a few days relaxing."

"So," Alex asked eagerly, "where are we going to go? San Francisco? The Grand Canyon? New York?" She didn't much care *where* they went, actually, just as long as she could tell Louis at school the next day that they were going *somewhere*, and not just staying home.

"Well," her father replied, "I was thinking Las Vegas. The company has a special arrangement there with one of the hotels, which gives us a discount on rooms and so on."

"Las Vegas?" Alex's eyes opened wide.

"That's cool! They've got some terrific new attractions, I hear."

Her mother frowned. "You're not thinking of *gambling*, are you?"

"Of course not," he replied hastily. "I was thinking of the shows, and the attractions. And Lake Mead and Hoover Dam. It could be very instructive for Alex."

Alex grimaced; she wanted *fun*, not education! Still, she should be able to get *some* fun in. Her parents both seemed to be very keen on the plan, so after they had finished eating and cleared the table, Alex went over to tell Ray what they were doing.

Ray and his father were playing saxophone duets together. Both of them were very good at it, and Alex had to admire that they were so close to one another. And Ray was now almost as tall as Mr. Alvarado. Alex told them the news, and Ray grinned.

"Hey, that's great news, Alex. It's a shame I'm going to be stuck here on my own, though."

Mr. Alvarado grinned impishly. "Who says you have to be stuck here?" he asked. "I've got a few days off. How would you like to go to Vegas as well?"

"You mean it?" Ray asked, excitedly. "Hey, that would be way cool."

"Then let's do it," Mr. Alvarado decided. "I'll go and speak to George, and see if we can't stay in the same hotel. Then you and Alex can have fun together."

Alex couldn't help grinning happily. Not only a neat vacation, but Ray was coming, too! This was going to be terrific. There was nothing that could spoil this trip, absolutely nothing.

Or, at least, nothing that she could *see* . . .

CHAPTER 2

"I'm telling you, Ms. Atron, this leave request of Mack's is *very* suspicious." Lars Frederickson stroked his short, dark beard and stared at his boss in concern.

Danielle Atron was behind her large, impressive desk in her office at Paradise Valley Chemical. As always, she looked coolly elegant, in a trim business suit and an impeccably white blouse. She radiated efficiency and focus. Right now, she was focusing on Lars, and in a manner that would have made a lesser man's skin crawl.

"Lars," she said, with deceptive gentleness, "I've heard quite a few of your paranoid accusations against George Mack in the past. Not one of them has ever proven to have had an ounce of truth in it. Why should I believe that this latest one of yours is any better?"

"Because," Lars said, leaning forward intently, "he's going to Las Vegas."

Danielle raised one eyebrow. "And that is suddenly a forbidden city?" she asked. "Lars, he's going there because the company has a very nice deal with the owner of one of the hotels. It's something called a *business perk*. Mack is a good worker, and very loyal to the plant. I happen to agree that he deserves a few days off with his family."

"It's not the *city* that's the problem," Lars explained. "It's the fact that there is a delegation from Keystone Petrochemicals staying at the Tropicana at the same time that causes me concern."

Danielle frowned slightly at that. Keystone was one of their largest corporate rivals. "It's probably just a coincidence," she decided. "There must be a lot of people in Vegas right now."

"*Probably?*" Lars echoed. "And what about the new analysis formula that Mack says he can't *quite* get to work?" He spread his hands helplessly.

Danielle was anything but stupid. She caught his meaning immediately. "You think that he might have finished it, and is simply pretending that he hasn't, in order to sell it to Keystone?"

"It's a possibility," Lars said. "After all, no matter how loyal an employee he is, that formula could be worth a great deal of money. If he *has* been approached by Keystone, then it's possible that he's struck a deal. Besides which, even though Mack has been taken off the GC-161 project, I'm not convinced that he's stopped working on it. If this formula of his does what he's hoping, then it will be of great use in projecting some of the properties of GC-161."

Danielle looked frustrated. "These are nothing but suspicions," she snapped.

"I agree," Lars admitted. "I don't have any proof of it. But . . . can you take the chance that I'm wrong? Wouldn't it be better to have someone in Las Vegas, watching Mack's every move? Someone who could tell you if he meets with anyone from Keystone?"

He could see her considering every angle of the idea. Finally, she nodded. "Very well. I don't *really* believe that Mack would do what you're suggesting. But if there's even the *slightest* chance that he is, we have to take action." She reached for her telephone. "I'll arrange for a room for you on the same floor as Mack, under a false name, just to be safe. Go out to Vegas and keep a very careful eye on him. If you see anything at all suspicious, let me know." She leaned forward. "I'll trust you to handle it discreetly."

"You can rely on me, Ms. Atron," he assured her smugly.

Her face went icy. "And I don't want any mistakes made, or you will most definitely pay for them. Do you understand me?"

"Perfectly," Lars assured her. The thought of failure simply never occurred to him.

"Good." She smiled again. "Then I think you'd better go and pack. I'll let you know all the details before you leave."

Lars nodded and hurried from the room. He couldn't keep a little smile of triumph off his face. He was absolutely certain that he had Mack this time. His other suspicions about the man hadn't been proven, but he was convinced that Mack knew far more about GC-161 than he'd ever let on. And that he really hadn't stopped investigating it. The only possible explanation for his behavior was that he intended to sell that information to a rival company. And Lars was completely committed to making certain that this never happened.

Whatever it took, he'd make certain that Mack's little secrets would soon be his.

Alex was feeling on the top of the world the morning of the trip. She had really enjoyed watching the smirk being wiped off Louis's face when he had asked, again, what they were doing for the break. He couldn't keep the envy out of his voice, either. It had been fun taking him down a peg or two—not that this would last long. Louis always bounced back. But maybe it would stop him from teasing them all for a while.

She'd visited the library and checked out a couple of guidebooks, reading up on Las Vegas. The town had a fascinating history, mixing pioneers, Indians, mobsters, and celebrities. And she could hardly wait to see some of the shows and spectaculars put on for the entertainment of the visiting tourists. They sounded like fun, and she could hardly decide what she wanted to see first. Since children weren't allowed to stay in the casinos, the hotels had all evolved new and bigger spectaculars to lure families to Vegas, from *Star Trek* to white tigers.

This was *definitely* going to be fun. For once, she wouldn't have to keep looking over her shoulder, wondering if she was being followed or spied on. It would just be a nice, relaxing few days of enjoying themselves and spending money.

And even that, unusually, wasn't a problem. Thanks to her baby-sitting jobs and some money left from her birthday, Alex had more than enough for whatever she chose to do and see in Vegas. Nothing could possibly mess up this vacation!

On Friday evening, Annie came home. Alex greeted her with an enthusiastic hug, one that Annie was just as eager to share. It felt even better knowing that Annie had missed her, too. When they were alone, Annie shook her head, grinning.

"I'm amazed you haven't been exposed by now without me around to rescue you," she said.

Alex tossed her head and tried to look haughty. "I've managed quite well enough on my own," she replied. Then she broke down giggling. "But there were a couple of times I *really* wished you had been here to help me out. Still, there's nothing to worry about on this trip, is there? Nobody in Vegas knows us, and we don't have to hide from anyone. We can just enjoy ourselves."

Nodding, Annie pulled her familiar journal from her backpack. "But, since we've got time to spare, I think it's a good idea for me to catch up on my notes about you."

Alex groaned. "This is one thing I haven't missed a bit," she complained.

"Look on the bright side: you won't have to put up with it again until I come home for the end of term. Now . . ."

But that had been last night. This morning, nothing bothered Alex at all as she helped to pack the bags into the car. Mom was fixing an early breakfast, and they should reach Vegas in the early afternoon. Fingers crossed! This was going to be nothing but fun!

Ray waved at them from his driveway, where he was helping his father load their cases into their car. They would follow the Mack family the whole way, with just a stop midmorning. It was kind of like being a wagon train, Alex thought. Going the wrong way, of course, and without the perils the pioneers had faced. But still exciting!

Lars was already on the road, since he had much less to pack and nobody to wait for. He aimed to be at the hotel and established before the Macks arrived. This way, he'd be able to follow them from the second they reached Vegas.

Nothing they did would escape his sight. Nothing.

Alex had thought that the journey would never end. They had hooked up with Interstate 15, taking that straight into Nevada. Then had come miles and miles of desert. It was kind of spectacular in its own way, with jagged, bare rock formations and stunted growths of shrubs and cactus. But you could look at only so many rocks and stones and sand before getting bored. She had to fight to keep from asking: "Are we there yet?"

But end it finally did. The interstate took them

through an area that was greener and more built up—and with quite heavy traffic as they worked their way to the exit for the local roads. Alex was used to the peaceful, slow pace of Paradise Valley. This car-infested maze of streets and construction sites was like an alien world to her. But still an exciting one!

It was still early afternoon, so she couldn't get the effect of the lights. But she realized that after dark, Las Vegas was going to be spectacular. As it was, the various buildings looked impressive. Mr. Mack turned the car down Tropicana Boulevard, and Alex couldn't help acting like a tourist. Well, she *was* a tourist, so she had an excuse! On the right was the Excalibur, one of the places she definitely wanted to visit. In all the modern buildings, it was weird and fun to see a fantasy-styled English castle, with hundreds of tourists pouring in and out. Beyond that, and just slightly visible, was the huge black pyramid of the Luxor, another must for her. The car turned onto the Strip itself, heading north. On the left was the MGM Grand Hotel, and behind it the theme park. Alex remembered from her reading that this was the biggest hotel in the world and it certainly looked it. On the left was the Monte

Carlo, which had gone in for the classic Greek look, with interesting fountains and not much more for her.

More interesting was the Holiday Inn, with its roller coaster and Ferris wheel on the roof. It was just a shame that these weren't real, because they looked kind of fun.

Then her father turned in to the hotel, and the next stage of activity began. Finally, though, they were upstairs in their room, unpacking just the bare minimum that they had to. None of them wanted to hang around too long; all of them were eager to get busy seeing and doing things. Ray and Mr. Alvarado had the same idea, and all six of them virtually collided in the hallway.

"Let's grab a bite to eat first," Mr. Mack suggested. "And then we can decide what we want to see and do first."

"The Cyclone Coffee Shop," Alex suggested. It helped having read up!

The others agreed, so everyone headed for the Holiday Inn. The Cyclone was decorated to continue the Coney Island theme, and it was almost as if you were out on a beach there, instead of indoors in a very busy town. Alex had a cheese-burger and fries, while Ray went for a "garbage" pizza—every topping they had. They headed for one of the few empty tables, and started to compare notes on what they wanted to see first.

"Excalibur," Alex said firmly. "I want to see the Lipizzans." She was fascinated with the beautiful white horses that virtually danced in time with music.

"Luxor," Ray said, just as firmly. "I want to hit the Secrets of the Pyramid." Alex remembered that this was supposed to be a high-tech ride of adventure, and it certainly sounded neat. But it surely couldn't compare to the dancing horses!

"How about Circus, Circus?" suggested Annie, joining them. "A circus is always fun."

"Yeah, but it's not *now*," Ray argued. "I want special effects, not dancing horses."

"There's always the Mirage," Mr. Mack suggested. "White tigers, dolphins, and so on."

Everyone, it turned out, had their own ideas as to what they wanted to see. Mrs. Mack wanted Caesar's Palace, and Mr. Alvarado wanted to visit the Oz area of the MGM, since *The Wizard of Oz* was one of his favorite movies. The discussion took a while to work out, but they finally all agreed that they wanted to see the sea battle at the Mirage, and they decided to head up there first.

As they were all leaving the restaurant, Annie and Mr. Mack finally started talking about his work. Alex had known this was inevitable, so she was glad that Ray was with them. Annie could get sidetracked into a scientific discussion faster than anything else.

"A new mathematical representation?" she asked, amazed. "That sounds really cool. Is it Boolean?"

Alex didn't have a clue as to what more than one word in every three meant, but Annie was quite clearly getting worked up by her father's explanation of his work. And Mr. Mack, too, seemed to be enjoying telling her about it. It's what he had needed, after all—someone who could understand it to talk to. Alex rolled her eyes and grimaced at Ray.

"I figure we could lead those two anywhere and they'd never notice," she said. "They're off in their own private world."

"One I'm glad we're not in," he answered, grinning. "So, who are you going to root for— the British or the pirates?"

"The pirates, of course," Alex said. "Can't you

just picture it, Ray? Cutlasses and cannons! The wind in the rigging. Preparing to walk the plank. Fighting—" She broke off, hearing a distinct crash, and looked around.

Annie had been so intent on talking with her father that she really hadn't been watching where she was going. As a result, she'd collided with a young woman. Both Annie and the young woman had fallen, and their bags had opened, scattering things on the floor.

"Oh, I'm so sorry!" Annie exclaimed, blushing as she sat up again. "I wasn't watching where I was going."

"No," the other person replied. "It was my fault also. I was looking for my lunch partner, and didn't see you coming."

Both of them scrambled to pick up their belongings, and Alex helped. She snatched up Annie's notebook—which contained all of her scientific observations about Alex—and returned it to her sister. In a minute, each of them had their bags packed again, and was apologizing to the other.

Alex looked around, eager to be off. And then she stopped, puzzled.

Watching them was an odd young man. He

was tall and gangling, with blond hair that fell over his thick-rimmed glasses. He was staring intently at Annie and the young woman, and jotting down notes on a small pad he carried. Suddenly aware he was being watched, he looked up and locked his gaze with Alex's. Abruptly, he blushed, thrust the pad into a coat pocket, and hurried rapidly away.

What was all that about? Alex didn't have a clue. She had never seen the man before in her life. But he had definitely been watching them, and he seemed to have been making notes about the accident. Why? Was there something going on?

Was this some fresh trick that the plant had dreamed up to catch her?

After all, the plant had arranged for these Vegas vacation packages. Maybe it wasn't simply a nice gesture to their employees. Maybe it was because Danielle Atron had a new scheme to catch the unknown GC-161 kid. . . .

Had Alex unwittingly walked right into another trap?

CHAPTER 3

As the party wandered up the Strip toward the Mirage, Alex dragged Annie aside and told her what she had seen. "Maybe this is a trick of some kind," she suggested.

"Alex, you're just being paranoid," Annie replied. "You didn't use any of your powers in that accident, so whatever that guy wrote down, it couldn't have been about you. Maybe he's a reporter, and it's a slow news day. And he was probably not even watching us anyway. Maybe he was making notes about his own vacation, and was just embarrassed to be stared at by a pretty young girl." She shrugged. "I know I'm

27

usually the one to say *be careful,* but I really don't think it's likely that we'll run into any trouble here."

Alex was almost certain that the mysterious man had been watching them. The way he'd blushed and hurried off proved that. But Annie was right—she hadn't used her powers, so she couldn't be in any trouble. Could she? The more she thought about it, the more she realized that Annie was probably right, and she was just over-reacting. It was time to have fun, not to worry over a minor incident!

They reached the Mirage at about five o'clock. The next show was at five-thirty, but already the area was pretty crowded. It wasn't hard to see why, since this was both a popular show and a free one. There was a large lagoon in front of the hotel, and two ships "floating" in it, though only the *Hispaniola,* the pirate ship, was now visible. It was moored outside a small village. The action would begin soon, and everyone was getting into a festive mood.

"I think I'd better buy a guidebook," Annie said, as they found a pretty decent spot to watch the action. "I'd like to know what we're watching." She took her wallet from her bag and opened it. Then she frowned, and stared at it more closely. "This isn't my wallet," she said. She shook her head. "That woman I bumped into! She must have had the same wallet as me, and ours got switched."

Alex stared over her shoulder. "Bummer. There's not much chance of finding her to switch back." There was a driver's license in the wallet, and she saw a picture that looked like the young woman, and the name Liseta Lopez.

"Yes there is," Annie answered. "She was meeting someone for a late lunch. If I hurry back, maybe she'll still be there. Come with me, Alex?"

Alex hesitated. There should be time to get back and switch wallets before the show, but she didn't want to miss this one. On the other hand, she couldn't just refuse Annie. "Okay," she sighed. "But we'd better hurry."

After explaining quickly to their parents, the two girls hurried back to the Cyclone. Once there, they quickly scanned the room and both spotted Liseta Lopez over by one of the windows, talking with a middle-aged man.

"There she is," Annie exclaimed, and they quickly crossed the room to where she was sitting. "Liseta!" she called, holding out the wallet. "Our things got mixed up in the collision."

Liseta suddenly went red, and half stood. The man with her scowled and stared from her to Annie. "What is this?" he demanded. "You told me that your name was Carla."

"My *middle* name," the woman answered. "The one I prefer to go by."

Alex was puzzled. There was something very odd here. The driver's license didn't show any middle name. And why was Liseta so uncomfortable? She watched as the woman and Annie exchanged wallets, unable to fathom this.

"Let's go, Alex," Annie said, grabbing her sister's arm. "We've just got time to catch the show if we rush."

"Yes," Alex agreed. "But—" And she stopped, really bothered this time.

The same odd man in thick glasses was watching them from the doorway, and he was again making notes in his book. As she saw him, he saw her, too. He whirled and rushed away.

"It's that man again!" Alex exclaimed. "He was watching us and making notes."

"Alex, are you sure?" Annie asked. "We've only just got time to go back to the show, but if you really think there's something happening, maybe we should investigate."

Alex considered the option in her mind. She really *didn't* know that there was anything wrong. Just a little odd at worst. And she *did* want to see the show. "It's probably nothing," she decided. "Let's go."

Allowing herself to be hurried along, Alex glanced over her shoulder. Liseta—or Carla— was arguing with her dining companion. What was going on here? This whole thing was making absolutely no sense at all to Alex. But it wasn't really her problem, was it? What was the young woman up to? Why had her wallet led her to argue with her date? And who was that strange young man who was following them around?

Did it have anything really to do with her? Alex shrugged mentally. Probably not. Life didn't always make perfect sense.

They made it back to the Treasure Island setting just in time to catch the opening of the show. As the pirates started to unload their ill-gotten gains, the British frigate *Britannia* came around the headland and challenged the pirates to surrender.

And then the battle began. Cannons roared, guns fired, men on ropes swung back and forth, fighting with cutlasses and hand to hand. It was all tremendous fun, and Alex soon forgot about the puzzling incident. It undoubtedly had nothing to do with her. Everyone was cheering along as the pirates managed to snatch victory from the jaws of defeat. In a final burst of explosions, the British ship was holed and sank to the bottom of the lagoon, to huge cheers from the crowd.

"Way to go!" Alex enthused.

"Wasn't that something?" Ray asked, his eyes shining, his grin wide and real. "Man, that was great. I'd love to be a part of that. Swashing my buckle all over the place."

"It was neat, Ray, really," Alex answered.

What Alex hadn't noticed was that Lars Frederickson was watching the group carefully from behind a large guidebook, his eyes peering thoughtfully at the Mack family. . . .

The family followed most of the tourists back down the Strip to the other show. Here was the next of the free shows. Outside the hotel and fronting another lagoon was a huge artificial volcano.

Once again, quite a crowd was gathering to watch the next show.

"So, you see," Mr. Mack was finishing explaining to Annie, "that's how the numeral spread will work."

"That's brilliant, Dad," Annie replied. "A real breakthrough."

"Except that I haven't been able to figure the final factor," her father answered. Then he frowned. "Wait a minute, though . . . Explaining it to you has helped me to clear some of the fog from my own mind. Quick, let me borrow your notebook."

"My notebook?" Annie's eyes caught Alex's in alarm. That was where she kept all of her data about Alex!

"The one in your pack," Mr. Mack said. "Hurry!"

With no option, Annie took out her book, and turned to the last page. Mr. Mack whipped a pen from his pocket and started to scribble on the paper furiously. Alex peeked over his shoulder, making certain that there was nothing about her already on the page. But Annie had chosen carefully, and there were just unintelligible formulas there that their father was jotting down at feverish pitch.

"There!" he exclaimed triumphantly. "That's the final factor. Now I've worked it out. Thank you, Annie!"

"My pleasure," Annie replied, reading what her father had written. "You've integrated chaos theory and fractal planning wonderfully."

"Say *what?*" asked Ray, completely lost. "It looks like an airsick spider scribbled on the paper to me. What does it all mean?"

"It's a tool, Ray," Mr. Mack explained proudly. "It predicts apparently random events."

At that moment, the volcano erupted. It appeared to be hurtling gouts of fire and lava into the air. Everyone in the audience either screamed, laughed, or applauded, as the volcano blew its top in a spectacular fashion.

"Like that!" Mr. Mack explained. "It looks random, but if I applied my formula, I could tell you where every last drop of that lava would land."

"*Inside* the safety barrier, I hope," Mrs. Mack said with a smile.

Alex could see that what her father had done was probably brilliant, but she didn't see the point of it. "Does it do anything that's useful?" she asked. "To everyday life, I mean," she added hastily, not wanting to sound rude. "Or is it just for predicting lava splatterings?"

"Oh, no," her father assured her as the crowd started to break up. "It can be applied to any kind of event that looks random. I developed it to help me predict the reactions of chemicals, but it can be used in many other ways."

Mr. Alvarado concentrated on this explanation. "What about roulette wheels?" he suggested. "Could you predict what number would win?"

Alex's father thought for a moment. "You know," he said slowly, "I do believe that it would, yes. I'd have to see what numbers come up during, say, a five-minute run. But after that, I ought to be able to predict the following sequence using my formula."

"Then what are we waiting for?" Mr. Alvarado asked eagerly. "Let's go and hit the tables. We could make some serious money if you're right."

"Oh, no!" said Mrs. Mack firmly. "George, you promised you wouldn't gamble. It's setting a bad example for the girls."

Her husband nodded in agreement. "Besides, it wouldn't be right to use it. It would be like cheating. I'd have an unfair advantage over everyone else."

Mr. Alvarado shook his head. "It wouldn't be gambling or cheating," he insisted. "It would be a scientific experiment. Look, George, you want to know whether your formula works, don't you? You wouldn't want to go back to your lab and find out you were wrong, would you?"

"No, I don't suppose I would," Mr. Mack admitted.

"Then just give the tables here a spin," Ray's father pleaded. "That way, you'll know if it will work, won't you?"

Mr. Mack considered it. "Let me sleep on it," he said, finally. "It will work just as well tomorrow as it would now. I'm really not sure it would be ethical to do it."

Mr. Alvarado sighed, but nodded. "Okay, George. But I just hope you remember that it's important to try out experiments."

Alex took Ray to one side. "Boy, your father is suddenly interested in scientific research," she commented.

Ray shook his head. "I think he's more interested in making some money on the tables, to be truthful. He's just trying to get your dad to go along with it." Ray frowned. "Do you think your dad really can do what he says? I've heard that people have been trying to work out a system to win at Vegas for decades, and none of them have ever succeeded."

"None of them have ever been my father," Alex said proudly. "If he thinks his formula will work, then I'll bet it will. He knows what he's talking about."

"Well," Ray said, grinning, "maybe we can all go home this weekend as millionaires, then."

Alex hadn't thought that far ahead. She realized that maybe Ray had a point. If her father *could* predict what number would come up next on the roulette wheel, then he really could make a fortune by betting on it. He really might be able to win millions of dollars. . . .

And would *that* be nice!

Lars scowled to himself as he watched the Mack family heading off for their next piece of blatant tourism. He was sure that this was just a smokescreen, to cover up Mack's *real* intentions here. He'd seen how Mack had scribbled something down in a book that Annie was carrying in her backpack. He'd been too far away to make out what had been written, but Lars was willing to bet anything it was that formula that Mack supposedly hadn't finished.

Which meant that his next move would have to be to get his hands on that book and uncover all its little secrets. If the formula was in it, who knew what else Mack might have noted inside it? He had to get hold of that book somehow. He was sure it would lead him to some interesting revelations about GC-161.

CHAPTER 4

Alex awoke the following morning feeling glorious. The previous night they'd taken in Siegfried and Roy's show. That had been incredible. The beautiful but dangerous white tigers, the weird tricks, the light show, the dragons, and fantasy adventures—it had all been absolutely fantastic. She'd been completely caught up in the spell that the two illusionists cast over the entire audience.

And she felt a little less paranoid this morning, too. Maybe Annie was right, and that odd young man wasn't really watching them. She *could* be making a mountain out of a molehill. And that Liseta Lopez . . . Okay, she had behaved a little oddly, but she seemed to have been very nice. And they weren't likely to run into her again anyway. Annie was right: she should stop worrying about things, and just relax and enjoy their time in this great town.

Alex couldn't help smiling when she realized that she'd actually woken up before Annie for once! It was the excitement that made her do it, and she didn't intend to waste a single minute of the day. "Wake up, lazy," she said, grinning, as she shook her sister in the next bed. As soon as Annie was awake, Alex went to take her shower and then got dressed.

Her parents were up by now, too, and the four of them decided to grab a buffet breakfast. They tapped on the Alvarados' room door, and Ray opened it almost immediately.

"You're all ready, too?" he asked cheerfully. "We'll be right with you."

Over breakfast, Mr. Alvarado brought up the question that Alex was wondering, too. "So, George, what's it going to be about your scientific experiment?"

Mr. Mack glanced at his wife. "Barbara and I have talked it over," he replied. "And we've agreed that I can use a hundred dollars to see if my theory is correct. If I'm wrong and lose it, then the experiment is off. If I'm right, we'll continue it for a while."

"Sounds good to me," Mr. Alvarado replied, rubbing his hands together.

"This sounds like fun," Ray said. "I'd love to watch a millionaire at work!"

"I'm afraid that's not possible, Ray," Mrs. Mack pointed out. "You're not allowed to stay in the gambling rooms unless you're over twenty-one. That means that all three of you will have to find something else to do with yourselves."

"Yes," Mr. Mack agreed. "You'll be on your own. Now, I know I don't have to tell you to be careful—you're all very alert and sensible people—but you have to take care."

That didn't make a whole lot of sense to Alex, but she got the rough gist of what her father meant. It was a shame that they couldn't watch him in action, but the upside of things was that the three of them could do whatever they liked, without the adults making all the decisions for once. Loose in Vegas—sounded like a formula for fun to her!

"Anyway," Mr. Mack finished, "we'd like to

see you back at the casino for lunch at one. Otherwise, the three of you are free to do as you like."

"All right!" Ray said happily.

"We'll be careful," Annie promised.

"And we'll have fun," Alex added.

They all headed for the casino that Mr. Alvarado had picked out. "Remember," he told them. "Meet us here at one."

"Definitely," Annie promised. "I'll make sure the two maniacs stay in line."

Mr. Mack patted her hand. "We know you will, Annie."

Alex rolled her eyes. Like they needed Annie to baby-sit them! Still, if it made the adults feel happier, fine. She turned to go and then stopped in surprise.

Walking in through the casino doors was Liseta Lopez again. And she had a different man with her. This one was short, slightly plump, and well-dressed. He had dark hair and a round face. Several feet behind them walked a dangerous-looking taller man.

And, across the room, the blond man with the glasses and notepad was watching the Macks again.

All of Alex's good humor evaporated. She *hadn't* been imagining things! That blond man *was* watching them for some reason! And how did Liseta Lopez come to be in the same place as the Macks again? Could it just be coincidence? She grabbed Annie's arm. "Don't make it obvious," she hissed. "But look at that man by the planter over there. It's the one who was watching us yesterday."

Annie snuck a look, and frowned. "You're right," she agreed. "And he's very carefully not looking in our direction. Alex, I'm sorry. You may have been right after all. This looks awfully suspicious to me."

At that moment, Liseta and her friends walked past them. Liseta glanced at the girls and stiffened slightly. She definitely recognized them. But then she blanked her face and walked past without a word. Annie had half opened her mouth to say hello, and then closed it again. They watched the Lopez party follow the Macks and Mr. Alvarado into the casino.

"Well." Annie snorted in disgust. "So maybe we didn't meet in the most cheerful circumstances, but there was no need for Ms. Lopez to act like she didn't know us."

Alex had a creeping feeling in her stomach. "Something odd is going on here, Annie," she said. "There're too many coincidences for my liking."

Ray nodded. "Yeah. There's an old saying: Once is happenstance; twice is coincidence; three times is enemy action."

"An old saying?" Alex asked. "Where did you hear that?"

"*Goldfinger*," Ray replied smugly. "And we've run into that blond guy with the notebook three times now. And this is a big, crowded town."

"It's not *that* big," Alex argued. "And if he's hanging around tourist spots—well, so are we."

"There's a lot of tourist spots," Annie pointed out. "Is it really coincidental that he's in the same ones we are?" She chewed at her lower lip. "There's one way to find out," Annie said decisively. "Let's head over to Caesar's Palace to check out the shops, and then head for the MGM Theme Park. If he follows us, then we'll know he's after us, and we can make plans."

"And if he doesn't?" Alex asked.

"Then we can shop!"

Lars slid through the assembled crowds and followed George Mack into the casino. He looked around carefully, trying to see if any Keystone Petrochemical employees were there. Then he almost smacked himself on the head. As if they'd wear their convention badges to a clandestine meeting with Mack! No, they'd contact him here somehow if they could. It was a smart move, planning a meeting in a public place. Everything would look completely coincidental to an unsuspecting person. But Mack wasn't going to fool Lars Frederickson that easily. He'd watch Mack like a hawk, and see what happened.

It was a shame that Annie wasn't here, too, but she wasn't old enough for the gaming rooms. Lars wanted to get his hands on that book very badly, but he could wait. The family would have to join up again at some time in the day, and then he'd figure out some way to sneak the book.

And then a dreadful thought came to him: Mack had written his formula down in the book, and Annie now had it! Was *she* the one who was going to hand it over to Keystone, while Mack was just a diversion? Was this casino thing simply to keep anyone following him focused on Mack, and ignore Annie?

Now Lars was in a quandary. Should he stay and watch Mack, or should he go after Annie?

After a moment, he realized that he had no choice: he had to stay here. He didn't have a clue where the kids had gone. It was best to stay here, and then maybe follow her later if he was sure she still had the book.

Uneasily wondering if he'd been conned into making the wrong decision, Lars settled down to watch George Mack. He had gone to the roulette wheel, and was watching it intently. It didn't make any sense to Lars, because Mack hadn't placed a bet. What was going on here?

The Forum Shops were stunning, and not simply for what was in them. Alex could hardly believe the place. There was a huge marble-looking archway that had to be about fifty feet tall. When you went through that, you were in the main street. The shops were amazing, and there were statues everywhere. The ceiling was painted to look like a sky scene, and there was a large dome in the center. Below this was an astonishing fountain, with lots of statues of various gods on it. Alex wasn't quite sure who they all were, but Jupiter and Venus were really obvious.

"Gucci," said Annie, almost in awe.

"Field of Dreams," said Ray, staring at a sports memorabilia store.

"West of Santa Fe," Alex said, dreamily picturing herself in a cowboy hat. It was hard to decide where to begin. They all looked like they could be fun to browse. Though, given some of the prices, browsing was probably all they could afford!

Alex glanced back, but there was no sign of anyone following them. Had the blond man given up? Or was he just hiding well? The only thing they could do was to check behind them every now and then and see if they could catch him out. So, far from reluctantly, she gave herself over to shopping.

An hour or so later, they decided to take a break from the stores. Alex had picked up a CD at the Virgin Megastore, and Ray had a baseball card he'd been looking for. Annie had a new top she'd fallen in love with, and they were all getting a little intimidated by the prices of some of the stuff.

"Let's do the rides," suggested Ray. "I want the Haunted Graveyard!"

The Motion Simulator Cinema Rides were downstairs, and Alex was keen to try them out, too. They ended up choosing a double, of the Space Ride and the Haunted Graveyard. The large-screen action was combined with moving seats that made it feel like you were really there, even more so since it was a 3D ride. Alex had a blast, howling and screaming with everyone else.

This was what she called a vacation!

Barbara Mack wasn't at all sure she understood quite what it was that George was doing. Science had never been her strong suit; she was more creative than scientific, more like Alex. But her husband seemed to be certain that this formula of his would work, and she knew how important it was for him to try it out. She didn't exactly approve of gambling; it seemed to her that the message of gambling was that you could make money without actually working for it, and she didn't care for this idea. It made people lazy and greedy.

And, she knew, pretty often it made them flat broke. The number of pawnshops and loan stores she'd seen on the way here hadn't reassured her. She knew that a lot of people could get really seriously into debt because of gambling. They thought their luck was bound to change, when it was quite obvious that the only ones who always made money at the tables were the people who owned them.

Still, George had promised her that he'd bet only a hundred dollars and no more, and she knew that he meant it. That couldn't do any harm, surely? And if it made him happy, she'd be glad to see him lose it. Of course, he was convinced that he couldn't lose.

He was doing some mental arithmetic now. "Seventeen," he said softly, as the ball spun around the wheel. The three of them watched it intently.

"Seventeen," the croupier announced, as the ball stopped. He began to draw in the chips and pay out the one person who'd won.

"That's amazing!" Barbara said, impressed with her husband.

"No, it's science," he assured her. He made another calculation. "It'll be twenty-six next," he told her, pushing his hundred dollars' worth of chips onto that square.

Barbara felt a pang of uncertainty and loss as he did so. "Are you sure?" she asked.

"Absolutely," he assured her.

The other players had bet, and then the man

spun the wheel before releasing the ball. Barbara couldn't take her eyes off it as it whirled around the inside of the wheel. As it started to slow down, she was willing it to go into 26, knowing that this was silly, but feeling a knot of excitement and panic in her stomach.

"Twenty-six," the croupier said, and pushed a pile of chips across to them.

"You did it!" Barbara exclaimed, throwing her hands in the air. "George, you did it!"

"Er, yes," her husband admitted. "But we have to keep on playing to make certain this wasn't just a fluke." He pushed the pile of chips over to 35.

Some of the other players stared at him. They were obviously wondering if he was just guessing, or whether he might somehow know something. They all placed their own bets. Barbara knew it had something to do with colors, and odds and evens and so on, but she wasn't very good with rules for this game.

And then the wheel and ball were spinning again. She stared at it, her nerves tingling with excitement. Could George do it again?

"Thirty-five," the man announced. Barbara squealed with delight as he pushed a larger stack of chips over to George. She had no idea how much this represented, but it was obvious that her husband was winning big-time.

People started to drift over to see just what was going on.

Alex was relieved to discover that there was no sign of the man who'd been watching them when they went over to the MGM Theme Park. The park was filled with fascinating rides, and she threw herself into enjoying them. The Lightning Bolt roller coaster, the Deep Earth Exploration, the white-water rafting . . . all pure fun.

Then it was time to head back to the casino to join the adults for lunch. Ray kept up a stream of conversation that Alex simply let wash over her. Ray was having a great time—and why not?

At the casino, they discovered that their parents were waiting for them, all three of them very happy. When Mrs. Mack saw them, she almost squealed.

"George is doing wonderfully!" she exclaimed. "His formula really does seem to be working."

"That's great, Dad," Annie said. "I'm so glad for you. This represents a major breakthrough."

"It also represents major bucks," Mr. Alvarado said. "How much is it so far, George?"

"About ten thousand dollars," Mr. Mack replied. "But that's not the point. The point is that my theory is holding up."

"I'll say," Annie exclaimed. "So, are you going back after lunch?"

"Probably for a while," Mr. Mack answered. "I'd like to try a different wheel, and see if it works in just the same way. When you're doing a scientific survey, you have to eliminate all random factors. For all I know at the moment, this theory might work only on the one wheel."

"By all means, let's spread it around," Mr. Alvarado agreed. "The more, the merrier—especially when it comes to Vegas."

They had lunch at the Flamingo Hilton, and Alex let the conversation wash over her as she sampled the buffet table. She enjoyed her food, and being off her feet for a while. Ray went back for thirds, and nothing seemed to bother him. Well, he had the right attitude. They were here to have fun, and that's what they were going to do.

Mrs. Mack patted Alex's hand. "Are you enjoying yourself, dear?"

"Definitely!"

Her mom smiled. "Well, we're all having fun. It was a marvelous idea that you had, and I'm glad you suggested a vacation."

"Me too!"

After lunch, they headed back to the casino, while Ray and Annie were arguing over where to go next. As their parents went back to the tables, Alex looked quickly back over her shoulder.

The blond man with the notebook was back again, watching them intently.

CHAPTER 5

Alex had gone through quite enough of this. She felt sick again as she saw this odd watcher. She could no longer doubt that he was after them for some reason. But why? There was only one thing to do, and that was to confront him and get a look in his notebook. That way, she could discover what he was after, and what he thought he knew.

Before she could point him out to Ray and Annie, though, a familiar voice said: "Ms. Mack! Hello again!"

It was Liseta Lopez, this time smiling and friendly. Alex did a double take. What was she doing here? Then she remembered that Liseta had been here earlier in the day, when she had snubbed them. Her mood seemed to have changed now.

Annie smiled at the young woman. "Hi again. I didn't think you remembered me."

"But of course I did!" Liseta protested. "You returned my wallet, with a lot of items in it that are important to me. Souvenirs of my family in Guatemala."

"You didn't seem to remember us this morning," Alex said dryly.

Liseta looked apologetic. "Ah. That must have been before I put my contacts in. I'm almost blind without them."

For some reason, this didn't ring true to Alex, but she wasn't going to argue. She had more important matters to worry about than this strange woman. She glanced around and saw that the blond man was still in the corner, watching them carefully. As Annie and Liseta chatted about Liseta's hometown, Alex nudged Ray.

"Our watcher's back," she murmured quietly. "I think it's time we got a look at what he's doing, don't you?"

Ray glanced back, and frowned as he, too, saw the man. "Yeah. Do you have a plan?"

Alex grinned. "I think a frontal attack and a little levitation might do the trick," she said. "Let's march right up to him."

"I'm game," Ray agreed. "Uh, Annie, excuse us for a couple of minutes, will you?"

"Sure, Ray." Annie turned back to Liseta. "So, you came to America to earn money to send back to your family?"

Annie was occupied, and, with luck, would keep Liseta from realizing that anything was going on. Alex and Ray marched across the lobby, directly toward the blond man in glasses.

He didn't seem to realize what they were doing until almost the last minute. Then he flushed red, whirled around, and rushed away, slipping his notebook in his pocket. Shielded by Ray, Alex sent out a telekinetic burst that lifted the notebook back from the man's pocket and flipped it to the floor. Ray scooped it up as they went past, and then the two of them diverted to an alcove.

"You'd make a great pickpocket, Alex," Ray said. "That was nicely done. I'm sure he didn't even notice."

"Well, let's see what we've got." Alex leaned over Ray's shoulder as he opened the pad up.

The handwriting was neat and tiny, and obviously abridged. "Target (B) met young woman (G) for conversation," the final line read.

"I don't get it," Ray said, puzzled. He started to read other entries. "Targets A and B to casino. Family (G-L) there again."

"We need to find out who those letters stand for," Alex told him. "Then maybe we can work out what this means."

"It means," said a very nervous voice, "that you're reading *my* property."

Alex and Ray looked round and saw the blond man staring at them, his face a mixture of worry and annoyance. Alex blushed in embarrassment, but their watcher seemed to be more embarrassed than she and Ray were.

"Could I have my notes back, please?" he asked, holding out his hand, which was shaking slightly. Ray started to give them back, but Alex stopped him.

"Not until you tell us just what's going on," she said firmly. "Why are you following us around? And what are you making notes about?"

"You?" The man blinked, and looked confused. "I'm not following *you*. I'm following *her*." He nodded toward Liseta, who was still chatting with Annie on the other side of the lobby.

"Her?" Alex felt a tremendous sense of relief. This *wasn't* some new plan of Ms. Atron's, then! "But why are you following her?" Now that she thought about it, she had only seen this nervous young man whenever Liseta was around, so he was most likely telling the truth.

"I don't know if I should tell you," the man answered. "It's confidential."

Ray had caught on now. "If you want your notebook back," he said, "then you'll talk."

The man glanced at where Liseta and Annie were chatting. They moved off together toward the ladies' room. "All right," he agreed, sighing. "I suppose I have no choice. But this is very confidential, okay?"

"Okay," Alex and Ray both chorused.

The man swallowed nervously, and then said: "My name is Sam Ace, of the Ace Detective Agency." He pulled his wallet from his pocket, and opened it to show them his license. He was so nervous, though, that he dropped the wallet.

Ray caught it before it hit the floor, and handed it back to Sam.

"No kidding?" Ray asked. "That's pretty neat."

"Well," Sam admitted, hanging his head slightly, "it's not really Sam *Ace*; it's Sam Spacey. But nobody would hire the Spacey Detective Agency, so I changed it to sound better. But I really am a private investigator."

"Neat," Alex said. She couldn't help liking him. He seemed so sincere, and . . . well, something of a klutz. "I'm Alex Mack, and this is my best friend, Ray Alvarado. So why are you following Liseta Lopez?"

"It's not so much her as the man she works for," Sam replied. He managed to replace his wallet in his pocket on the third attempt. "Do you know who that man she was with this morning is?"

"Not a clue," Ray answered cheerfully.

"That's Big Al Drury," Sam answered.

Alex shook her head. "Never heard of him. Is he some kind of gangster?"

"Not exactly," Sam admitted. "There really aren't many big crooks left these days in Vegas. But Big Al is a medium-sized crook. He runs

59

scam games, and your Ms. Lopez is one of his gang."

"She's not *our* Ms. Lopez," Alex said. "It's just that my sister Annie ran into her yesterday." She explained about the wallet mix-up. "And she just ran into us again, and now she's acting friendly all of a sudden."

"It's probably the prelude to a scam," Sam answered. "You see, Big Al has this really neat one going right now. I'm working for a client he ripped off, and trying to get proof that he's a crook. See this button on my lapel?"

Alex peered at it. It said: I ♡ Las Vegas. "What about it?" she asked.

"It's a hidden camera," Sam explained proudly. "I'm filming whoever Big Al or Liseta meets, and I'm hoping to get evidence to convict them."

"So what do they actually *do*?" Ray asked. He examined the hidden camera with interest. This was definitely his style. Alex could see him imagining himself as an undercover agent. . . .

"It's one of the oldest tricks in the book," Sam answered. "But there's always somebody who falls for it. Liseta plays a few games in the casino, where she and Big Al select a likely victim.

Since she's young and pretty, they tend to go for middle-aged men, who are flattered when Liseta seems to like them."

Alex was starting to understand what was happening. "That man we saw her with yesterday!" she exclaimed. "The one she gave a fake name to."

"Right," agreed Sam. "He was going to be her next victim, but you and your sister managed to spook him off. I was sure I was going to get evidence there."

"But we ruined it by accident," Alex said. "I'm sorry, Mr. Ace."

"Call me Sam," he answered. "It's okay, you had no way of knowing, and there's still a good chance I'll get them. What Liseta does is to tell the men that she's a poor immigrant from Guatemala—which happens to be true, by the way. And then that she's won a lot of money at the tables. The problem is, she claims, that she's here illegally, and can't collect her winnings without getting deported back to her home country. That's a lie; she's a perfectly legal alien, but of course these men believe her. She then asks them to collect her winnings for her, and offers to split them fifty-fifty."

"Sounds pretty generous of her," Ray commented.

"It does," agreed Sam. "That's why so many people fall for it. The neat part comes when she says that she needs the man to prove his good faith by putting up some of his own money—say ten thousand dollars—to be held by a third party until the man collects the money."

And now Alex got the point. "And I'll bet that third party is Big Al, and he and Liseta just slip off with the cash, leaving the man they've conned with a ticket that isn't worth anything."

"That's right," Sam agreed. "And the man generally feels too embarrassed to go to the police, so he just writes the experience off, and Liseta and Big Al get away with it. After each scam, they hide for a couple of weeks until the gambler's left town, and then they resurface and try again. Well, my client was fooled, and he doesn't want to press charges himself because he's afraid it'll make him look silly. So he's paying me to track Liseta and Big Al and get proof that they're crooks." He lowered his voice slightly. "This is my first really big case, guys, so it's very important to me. I've *got* to succeed."

Alex felt bad for him. He was so likable, but

at the same time, kind of spacey, just like his name. If she had been able to spot him so easily, then probably Big Al and Liseta had, too. They might even have been deliberately meeting with the Macks to try and throw him off-track. She handed his notebook back to him. "Well, good luck," she said. She had a suspicion he was going to need it. "We'll try to stay out of the way from now on."

"Yeah," Ray agreed. "We don't want to mess up your case."

"Thanks, guys." Sam smiled at them both. "Okay, I've got to go now. Your sister and Ms. Lopez are coming out. I don't want her to see me with you two. 'Bye." He hurried off, trying to hide himself again.

"He's going to need more than luck to nail those crooks," Ray said. "He's really nervous, did you notice that?"

"Yes," Alex admitted. "This is so important to him that it's freaking him out, I think. But it's nothing we can do anything about. I'm just relieved it wasn't another one of Ms. Atron's plots." She saw her sister wave good-bye to Liseta, who left the casino. Alex and Ray grinned at one another as Sam slipped out after her.

Annie came over to join them. "That Liseta is really nice," she commented. "Did you know she's here in America to earn money to send back to her family? They live in Guatemala, and their average income is only three dollars a *month*. It's terrible that people have to live like that."

Alex sighed. "Your *friend* is a crook, Annie," she informed her sister. "She preys on middle-aged men and cons them out of their money. *That's* how she supports her family back home. *If* she has one."

"What?" Annie looked stunned. "Are you sure of that?"

"Absolutely." Alex told her sister everything that Sam had related to her and Ray.

"You didn't let her anywhere near your money, did you?" Ray asked. "I'd check and be sure you've still got it, if I were you."

"You don't think she'd rob *me*, do you?" But Annie pulled off her backpack and rummaged inside it until she found her wallet. She checked it, and sighed with relief. "It's all here," she replied. "Look, maybe this Ace isn't so hot, and he's got things mixed up? Liseta seems like a real nice . . ."

Her voice trailed away. Alex frowned. "What is it, Annie?"

"My notebook," Annie said, searching through the pack. "It's not here! She must have taken *that!*"

Alex stared at her sister in horror. The crooks had Annie's notebook—and all her scientific data about Alex! If they read the book, they'd know Alex's secret. And there was no way they'd keep quiet about it when they could make a fortune for themselves by selling her to Danielle Atron!

CHAPTER 6

Barbara Mack could hardly keep her excitement bottled up as she watched George bet on the new roulette wheel. He'd chosen 23, and 23 came up. "George, you're wonderful!" she exclaimed.

"It's just scientific application," he murmured modestly, but he was flushed with excitement, too.

One of the onlookers gave him a big smile. He was a short, dark-haired, well-dressed man. "You got a system, pal?" he asked.

Mr. Mack blinked and then nodded. "Well, not so much a system as a scientific formula," he explained. "It enables me to predict random

events, such as the fall of the ball in the roulette wheel."

The man nodded at the pile of chips George
now had. "It looks to me like it works." He held
out his hand. "The name's Al Drury."

Mr. Mack shook it. "George Mack," he replied,
trying to concentrate on the spin of the wheel.
But the smaller man didn't seem inclined to
shut up.

"Is this system of yours a secret, or would you
be willing to share it?" Mr. Drury asked. "I
could make it worth your while."

"Oh, no, I'm afraid it's a trade secret," Mr.
Mack explained. "I've developed it for the company that employs me, and I don't think they'd
like me to just give it away to people. Besides, I
really don't think you'd be able to understand
it."

"Try me," Mr. Drury suggested.

Mrs. Mack didn't have a good feeling about
the man. He seemed a little creepy, but she tried
not to be judgmental. It was only reasonable that
people would be curious as to how George was
doing so well.

Giving up on playing for the moment, Mr.
Mack turned to Al Drury. "Well, it's an applica-

tion of Heisenberg's Uncertainty Principle," he answered. "It's just a matter of integrating this with chaos theory and then redefining the parameters to include coefficients such as air resistance, surface tension and . . ."

Mrs. Mack tuned it all out. She really couldn't follow the technical side of things that well, since it wasn't really her field. Judging from the dazed expression on Mr. Drury's face, it wasn't his, either. But now George was launched on an explanation, and it would take a great deal to stop him once he was in full flow. Mrs. Mack wandered off to the complimentary buffet to find a couple of finger sandwiches and some seltzer water. She wished Mr. Alvarado were still with them to chat, but he'd gone off to buy tickets for Michael Crawford's show. He was really into the musical scene.

"Annie, how *could* you?" Alex exclaimed. "That book could sink my life! And now those crooks have it!"

"Alex, I'm really sorry," Annie apologized. She looked totally distraught. "But I thought she was just being nice. I guess she really fooled me, didn't she?"

"Let's not argue about whose fault it is," Ray said firmly. "What's done is done. But we've *got* to get that notebook back before she has a chance to read it."

"Agreed," Alex said. "If they read those notes on me and go to Danielle, not only will they make a lot of money, but I may spend the rest of my life as a permanent test subject at the plant."

"But we don't know where she went," Annie pointed out glumly. "Alex, this is all my fault."

"It's not," Alex answered. "None of us had any reason to think Liseta was anything other than what she seemed to be. But we've got to find her. We'd better split up and search. If we don't find anything, we'd better meet back here in an hour and see if we can come up with a better idea." They rushed out of the casino into the crowded street.

"I'll go up the Strip," Annie decided. "Alex, you go down. Ray, you try down Harmon, and then back up Flamingo, okay?"

"Right." Alex turned and hurried down the Strip, her eyes darting from side to side as she went. All she needed to do was to spot either Liseta or Sam, since Sam was sure to be hot on her trail.

She didn't like to think about what would happen if she failed to get that book back. It was all the evidence that Ms. Atron would need to grab Alex and subject her to experimentation. Ms. Atron was dying to find the kid from the accident. To have the kid as a test subject was her greatest desire. She wanted to use GC-161 as a weight-reduction aid. She didn't have any idea of its *real* side effects.

But if she had Alex in her clutches, then she would test Alex forever. And Alex knew that she would not like the process at all.

She *had* to get Annie's book back at all costs!

It was like finding a needle in a haystack, though. And not just a simple haystack, but one that kept moving and shifting around. The crowds hid Liseta from view, and Alex knew that she didn't stand much of a chance of finding her.

As the hour wore on, she became more and more frantic. She'd checked out everywhere that she came to down as far as the Luxor, and then started back up the other side of the road. There were thousands of people, most of them enjoying themselves tremendously. There were hundreds of rides, but Alex was pretty sure that Liseta wouldn't be on one of those. She'd be meeting up with Big Al, obviously, but where? She checked out restaurants, cafés, and shops. She peered into casinos, but couldn't go any farther than the doors because of her age.

Nothing.

She was also trying to work out why Liseta would have stolen the notebook. She couldn't possibly have figured out what it contained. After all, the chances that Big Al might have heard of GC-161 were so slim as to be none. Then *why* had she taken the book? What else was in it but Annie's notes?

And then Alex realized what was going on. Big Al and Liseta had been in the casino when Dad was winning his money. And they must have suspected that he'd written down his formula in Annie's book! They must have realized that her father had a system to win at roulette, and they wanted the secret for themselves. Getting Annie's notes was just an accident.

Maybe, then, just *maybe*, they wouldn't understand them? They might just think that it was some school project Annie was working on. Or even a story? Alex was clutching at straws, but at the moment, there wasn't much else she could do. If she didn't get the book back, she could only pray that the notes wouldn't interest the crooks.

And then the hour was up, and she had no results at all. Frustrated, anxious, and scared, Alex made her way back to the casino. She hoped that one of the others had better luck than she did, but they were both waiting for her with glum expressions on their faces. She didn't have to ask them how they'd done.

"I'm doomed," Alex sighed, her stomach all twisted up. "Maybe, once they read the formula, they won't read the rest of your notes."

"Maybe," agreed Annie. "But I don't think we'd better count on that."

"Me neither," Ray added. "There's got to be *some* way to get that book back. So what do we do now?"

Annie glanced at her watch. "We've got a little more time, but then we have to meet our parents again. We could take another swing around town."

"It's hopeless, Annie," Alex said. "We'll never find her like this."

Annie suddenly nodded. "Alex, you're right. We won't. This is hopeless."

"Uh, Annie," Ray said, worried, "that's not exactly going to cheer Alex up, you know."

"I know." Annie grinned. "But I have an idea. Dad brought his laptop with him. It's in our room right now. I'll use it to try and hack into the hotels' databases. If I can find out where Big Al or Liseta are staying, then we can just go there and wait for them to show up."

Alex felt a slight surge of hope. "Do you really think you can do that?" she asked.

"I don't know, Alex," Annie admitted honestly. "But I've got to try, haven't I? It's a better chance than just walking around a town this size and hoping to trip over her." She smiled encouragingly at Alex. "Though maybe you and Ray should try that. There's not much help you can give me with the computer search."

"I guess," Alex said. She and Ray watched Annie hurry off back to their hotel room. "Well, Ray, I guess it's one more turn around town before we meet our folks for dinner."

Ray put a comforting hand on her shoulder. "Cheer up, Alex. We'll find the book. I know we will. You, me, and Annie are such a great team. Nobody will beat us. You'll see."

Alex appreciated his encouragement, but she

couldn't quite bring herself to believe it. Everything seemed to be so hopeless right now.

Lars squinted as he hurried after Annie Mack. His morning had been wasted watching George do nothing but play the roulette wheel. As he had come to suspect, his actions were just a diversion. It was his daughter, Annie, who was the important one. When the family had met up for lunch, Lars had grabbed a quick snack himself and then latched onto following Annie. She'd met up with a strange woman, and then hurried off on a pointless trip around various casinos and attractions.

Or had it been pointless? She had then hurried back to meet her sister and that neighbor of theirs at the casino, and now Annie was heading back to the hotel. She seemed to have something very firm in mind, and Lars knew that it had to be the transfer of the data he'd been expecting. All he had to do was to follow her and get that book from her bag before she could turn it over to anyone from Keystone. . . .

At the hotel, Annie went to the elevator. Lars loitered in the lobby, watching until the doors closed. Then he watched until the elevator she'd taken opened on the seventh floor. She'd gone to her room, as he'd expected. He took the next elevator up, and then hurried along to the Macks' little suite. She had to be inside there, and that meant that he needed to know what she was doing.

Lars went to the room next to the Macks'. This one was where the Alvarados were staying. He knew that they were out, so he should be safe. The locks were the magnetic key type, which were supposed to be burglar proof. Perhaps to the average man or crook they might be, but he was far from being average. He pulled a computer probe from his pocket. This looked a little like a hand calculator with a knife attached to it by wires. Lars slid the blade into the lock, and activated the small device.

It used electronic pulses to analyze the lock, looking for the correct sequence that would allow him access. After about thirty seconds, it beeped, and the door clicked. With a smile, Lars pushed open the door and slipped into the Alvarados' room. He hurried to the balcony, and then clambered across to the balcony of the Macks' room. Then he peered into the room.

Annie was at the table, bent over a laptop

computer. Her bag was on the floor by her feet. Lars checked the lock on the sliding doors, and saw that it was open.

He settled down to wait. All he needed was for Annie to leave the room for a few moments for any reason. Then he could slip inside and get everything he needed. Lars smiled happily to himself. The Macks thought that they could outwit everyone, but they weren't reckoning with Lars Frederickson's being wise to them.

He'd make certain that he'd get exactly what he needed. And then Mack would be out at the plant, and he would have all of the secrets of GC-161. . . .

"I'm doomed, Ray," Alex said again. They had been wandering about the streets for almost an hour, and there was still not a sign of either Liseta or Sam. The longer Annie's notebook was missing, the greater the chance that Alex would be discovered. She glanced at her watch. "I guess we'd better head back to the casino and meet our folks," she said reluctantly. "We'll tell them Annie has a stomach bug, and is resting. That should buy her the time she needs."

Ray nodded as they started back. "Do you think she can find out where the crooks are?"

"If anyone can, it's Annie." But Alex couldn't feel too hopeful. "On the other hand, if we don't get that book soon, it won't matter if she finds out where they are. All they need is time to talk to Danielle Atron, and I'm finished."

"Cheer up, Alex," Ray said. "I'm sure it won't come to that."

"Well, that's one of us who thinks that," Alex replied. They walked the rest of the way back in silence. Inside the casino, they waited in the lobby for their folks to emerge.

When the Macks and Mr. Alvarado appeared, there was another man with them. He looked rather dazed and confused as Alex's father shook his hand.

"Well, it was nice meeting you, Mr. Drury," he said. "I really enjoyed our little chat."

"Your little lecture, I think you mean, George," Mrs. Mack added, laughing. "Poor Mr. Drury's going to have a headache for a week, I think."

Alex grabbed Ray and dragged him behind a huge potted palm, barely able to contain her excitement. "Ray, that's Big Al!"

77

"You're right," Ray agreed, puzzled. "But so what?"

"He's been with my folks all afternoon," Alex explained. "So Liseta can't have given him the book yet! I'm still safe." She made her mind up fast. "Tell my folks that *I'm* the one with the stomach bug, and that Annie's taken me back to our room. And that we'll catch up with you all later."

"Okay," Ray agreed. "But what are you going to do?"

"I'm going to follow Big Al and try to get the book back," Alex explained. "This is our best chance."

"Alex!" Ray exclaimed. "It's too dangerous! The guy's a crook. He's probably carrying a whole arsenal hidden in his clothes."

"Not a chance," Alex answered. "Look how stylish they are. There's not an inch where he could be hiding anything. Ray, I'll be okay. But it's *vital* that you keep our folks from suspecting there's any trouble. You've got to make them believe I've barfed after all this morning's excitement. You can do it, I know you can." She grabbed Ray's arm again. "Al's leaving. Get over

78

there and distract our parents while I slip out after him!"

She could tell that he wasn't keen on leaving her, but he knew that she was right. With a reluctant nod, he hurried across the floor.

"Dad, Mr. and Mrs. Mack!" he said, heartily. "It's good to see you all! How are you doing at roulette?"

"Still ahead," Mr. Mack answered. "Where are the girls, Ray?"

Alex ignored them now, as Ray kept them busy. She shot out of the door, and saw Big Al disappearing down the street ahead of her. He was completely unaware that he was being followed, so she stayed back about ten feet, dodging in and out of the crowds. He seemed a little dazed; some people felt that way after Dad talked to them for a while. Alex loved her father, but she knew he had a habit of plowing ahead with what was important to him without worrying whether he was being understood or not.

Big Al turned into one of the hotels just ahead and headed for the elevators. He got into an empty car, and set it going. Alex hurried after him. She had to find out which room he was heading for, but how could she do that? He would arrive on his floor, and by the time Alex could take another elevator up after him, he'd be long gone.

Unless . . .

As soon as the elevator lights indicated that his car had stopped at the fourteenth floor, Alex leaned against the call panel and sent a careful bolt through the system. It was very difficult for her to control it, but she managed to use her zap to short out the door-opening button for a while. It wouldn't last more than a couple of minutes, but while it did, his car doors wouldn't open to allow him out. Alex took the next car up to the fourteenth floor, and then bolted outside. The doors to the other elevator hadn't opened, and she could hear someone banging inside. Her plan had worked! She dived into the alcove where the ice machine stood, and then looked back at the elevators. There was nobody in sight, so she sent another careful zap at the control panel.

The doors to Big Al's car suddenly opened, and he almost collapsed into the corridor. He turned and kicked the doors as they closed behind him, but obviously didn't suspect that the problem had been deliberate. Then he stomped down the hall to a room. Using his key, he entered it.

Alex dashed after him, and stopped outside the door. She could hear voices inside, so Liseta had to have been there, waiting for him. Looking both ways down the corridor, Alex saw she was still alone. Focusing her mind, she liquefied herself. Turning into a viscous liquid, Alex melted into a puddle of silver on the carpet, and then slid herself under the door and into Big Al's room.

In this state, her vision and hearing were a little odd. She heard echoes with every sound, and saw shimmering reflections around everything. But she could somehow still hear and see, even without eyes and ears.

Big Al's room matched his name. It was obviously very expensive and large, more like an office than a room. Big Al had taken off his coat and thrown it onto a four-poster bed, and he was now talking to Liseta at a desk in an alcove. Alex zipped across the floor behind them and into the palatial bathroom. There she returned to her normal state; she couldn't stay liquid for very long, and she didn't want to drain her strength unnecessarily. She might have to get out of here in a hurry!

"I don't like this, Mr. Drury," Liseta was saying, as Alex listened carefully. "It is one thing for me to cheat these men that you pick out. They are foolish and rich, and they can afford to lose their money. It is not so fair to steal from a nice family."

"Who asked you to do any thinking for yourself?" growled Big Al. "That idiot Mack has some kind of system that enables him to win at roulette. At this rate, he'll rack up tens of thousands of dollars in one day. That makes the money we normally get look like chicken feed, sweetheart, and I want in on it."

"I am *not* your sweetheart," Liseta answered. "I don't even like you."

"You don't have to like me," Big Al replied with a barking laugh. "Just as long as you do what you're told. You're only useful to me as long as you obey orders. And you know what will happen if you don't do exactly as you're told. But this game is bigger than anything we've ever done before. I had a talk with this Mack guy." He groaned slightly. "He almost talked both my ears off, but I couldn't make out what he was saying. It was all scientific nonsense. All I could understand is that he's got this formula that predicts where the roulette ball will end up. Now, did you get that book like I told you to?"

There was a short pause. Alex realized that Liseta didn't really want to turn it over to her boss. She clearly didn't like him very much. So why was she working for him? Alex had a suspicion that there was more to this than she'd thought.

"Yes," Liseta finally said. "Here it is."

Alex felt a surge of excitement and apprehension at the same time. She now definitely knew where Annie's notes were. Unfortunately, they were in the hands of Big Al. . . . She had to get them back before he could read the book, and that meant she needed some sort of distraction.

She looked wildly around the bathroom, hoping for inspiration. All she needed was to get them away from the book for a few minutes. . . . And then she had an idea. Using her powers, she turned on the faucets in the bathtub, and then started the whirlpool jets going. A quick zap then made all the lights come on, and start blinking on and off. Immediately, she morphed into her pool of liquid.

"What the—?" Big Al roared, and he dashed into the bathroom, Liseta following close behind. If they saw Alex, they must have taken her for a puddle on the floor. "What's going on here?"

"Everything's gone crazy!" Liseta exclaimed, as they both went to try to shut off the water.

Alex slipped out of the bathroom, and into the alcove where the desk was. Annie's book had been dropped on the table. Alex morphed back into her human shape and grabbed the book, sighing with relief. She was just about to morph back into liquid and escape under the door when she suddenly saw that there was someone on the balcony.

It was Sam, and he was trying to get a better view into the bathroom, to make out what was happening. Alex felt a flush of shock, wondering if he'd seen her morph. Then she realized that he probably couldn't have, since he was watching the bathroom, not the alcove where she crouched in hiding. He must still be trying to get evidence against Big Al! Alex silently wished him luck, and was about to morph to escape when she saw Sam miss his footing, and fall backward against the balcony railing. His foot kicked a pot, which crashed to the ground.

Alex realized with shock that Sam was way off balance. He was flailing his arms, but he was obviously going to fall. Without considering the consequences, Alex reached out with her teleki- netic powers and hauled him back to safety. Since he didn't know she was here, he might wonder how he'd been saved from certain death, but he'd never connect it to her.

Instantly she morphed, taking the book with her. But she didn't have a chance to run for it, because the noise from the balcony had alarmed Big Al. He rushed out in time to see Sam hop- ping to the next balcony.

"It's that idiot detective," Al growled. "He's stopped being amusing and is getting irritating. It's time to fix him once and for all." He snatched up a walkie-talkie from the desk, and then paused. "Hey! The book's gone! That fool must have snatched it somehow."

Alex saw a slight smile on Liseta's face. It was as if she wanted Sam to beat her boss somehow, which didn't make any sense to her at all. But Sam's arrival and clumsy accident meant that Big Al didn't have a clue as to what had actually been happening in his room. While he and Liseta were watching the balcony, Alex slithered across the floor and out of the door. Once in the corridor, she morphed back to her human form and raced for the elevator.

"Hey, you!"

Alex glanced over her shoulder and saw a burly man round the corner and start after her down the corridor. He had a walkie-talkie in his hand, and was obviously the man Big Al had been calling. For a second Alex considered trying to bluff it out, but she was carrying the book that Al was after. It wouldn't work. And she had no time to wait for the elevator.

She spun around and bolted for the stairs. She could hear the burly man thunder after her. He looked like a bodybuilder, and she had no doubts whatsoever that he could do her serious damage if he caught up with her. So she had to make certain that he didn't. As she pushed through the door to the stairs, she fired a quick zap at the lock to fuse it. Then she started down the stairs, two steps at a time. It was fourteen floors to the ground, and she hoped she could keep up this pace.

There was a crash as her pursuer hit the door, and then a second one as he hit it again and it flew open. Alex glanced back and saw the man start down the stairs after her. She had barely a floor's lead on him, and he was bigger and more athletic than she was.

This was going to be trouble.

Panting, her heart beating like crazy, Alex ran down the steps as fast as she could. Her legs were already starting to ache, and she was certain she could hear the man closing in behind her. Then she heard him yell into his walkie-talkie: "Cut her off at the third floor!"

Oh, no! There were more of Big Al's thugs in the building, of course, and one of them was going to get ahead of her! There was now no escape down the stairs.

She was trapped.

CHAPTER 7

Lars shifted position to avoid getting a cramp as he watched Annie carefully through the gap in the room's curtains. After about fifteen minutes, she suddenly leaped to her feet and yelled, "Yes!" Lars had no idea what she was doing, but it was obviously something important, and had to do with the computer. Then she hurried out of the room and into her adjoining bedroom.

Grabbing his chance, Lars slipped into the room. He glanced at the computer and saw that it had the name Al Drury and a fourteenth-floor room at a nearby hotel. That had to be the contact person that Annie was going to hand the book over to. Well, he'd put a stop to that! Lars grabbed Annie's backpack, and started to hunt through it.

In a few seconds, he realized that the book was no longer there. And then he heard Annie returning. Quickly, he replaced the bag and slipped into the half-open closet beside the desk. He held his breath, and listened as Annie shut down the computer and then grabbed her backpack and headed for the door. As soon as the door closed behind her, Lars emerged and hurried after her. He'd have to give her a short lead—it wouldn't do to be seen coming from the Macks' room—but he was sure he could beat her to the other hotel anyway. There he'd recover the book and get proof that the Macks were up to no good. This would finish George Mack at Paradise Valley Chemical forever!

Alex didn't know what to do for a moment. The burly man behind her was getting closer all the time, and now he had a friend waiting below to catch her! She couldn't keep going this way, that was for certain.

She rounded the stairs and started down the next flight, hearing the heavy footsteps above her. And, not far below, she heard a door open. That had to be the second man! She was down to the seventh floor now, and if he started up, she'd be trapped any minute.

Which meant it was time to be sneaky. As she rounded the next flight of stairs, she was out of view of her pursuer for a second, and she used that second to morph into liquid form. She huddled to one side of the stairs, trying to be inconspicuous. The man hurried past her without a glance—after all, he was chasing a girl, not a puddle!

Immediately, Alex slithered out of the stairwell and into the corridor on this floor. There was nobody in sight, so she reverted to human form and dashed over to the elevators, pressing the down button. She didn't have much time; any second the two men on the stairs would realize she'd given them the slip.

And then the elevator arrived, and she dived in. There was a family of Japanese tourists in there, all cameras, T-shirts, and dark glasses, chattering away. Alex gave them a quick smile and then mentally urged the elevator to go faster.

It stopped on the fourth floor, and two more

people got in. Alex had to fight to restrain her impatience and her nerves. The longer this took, the more likely it would be that she'd be intercepted.

And then they reached the lobby, and the doors opened. Alex decided to risk being rude, and pushed out fast, glancing around the lobby. She stiffened in shock as she saw the burly man heading for the elevators, a grim expression on his face. She didn't think he'd dare to grab her in public, but she wasn't willing to take the chance. All he really wanted, after all, was the book. He might be able to snatch it and run.

Alex turned and dashed the other way. Unfortunately, it was deeper into the hotel, which wasn't a very good thing. She had to get away from him somehow! And then she saw her chance—the ladies' room! He wouldn't dare follow her into that, so Alex plunged through the door, and then into a stall. There were several other women already in the room. Alex held her breath, and to her relief, the burly man didn't show up.

But now what? Big Al was bound to get Liseta to come in after her, so she couldn't stay here. And she couldn't leave through the door; Al's man would be waiting for that. Which left her just one option—through the drains. But that meant waiting for there to be nobody in the room. Would that happen?

Two of the women left together, chattering away. Alex waited impatiently. Were the other two ever going to leave? One was brushing her hair, the other touching up her mascara. Alex felt like screaming at them to hurry up, but she managed to restrain herself. It couldn't be long before Liseta arrived, and she *had* to be gone by then!

The third woman finally stopped fussing with her hair and left. That left just the one with the makeup problem, and she seemed to be settled in for life. She replaced her mascara, and took out a tube of lipstick. Alex winced. Would she never end? Alex simply didn't dare wait any longer. As the woman started to apply the lipstick, Alex tweaked it from her hand using her powers and sent it rolling across the floor.

The woman gasped and then chased after it. Alex morphed into liquid form, and poured herself down the nearest sink. As she did so, she heard the door to the rest room open, and saw Liseta walk in.

She'd barely made it in time! But there was no way that they could follow her now. All she had to do was to slide down the pipes until she came to an opening somewhere. Then she could revert to normal and simply walk away. Having her powers definitely came in handy at times.

Annie rushed over to the casino, hoping to be able to find Alex and let her know where Big Al was staying. But there was no sign of the family there. Annie glanced at the clock and realized that they must have gone for the afternoon break. Dad had said something about Rio's Carnival World Buffet, she remembered, so she headed for that.

By the time that she reached it, everyone was already leaving. Annie felt a growl of hunger in her stomach, but there was no time to eat right now. She saw her parents and the Alvarados, but no sign of Alex.

Ray spotted her first, and jumped forward. "Annie!" he said, loudly. "How's Alex feeling? Any better?"

Annie realized that this was the "reason" Alex was missing. "Much better," she said. "In fact, she's ready to be up and about again now. I thought we might go and join her."

"That's good news," her mother said. "I just hope that Alex doesn't overdo it again, though. You know how your sister can be."

"Oh, yes," Annie agreed fervently. "I know *just* how she can be."

"Well, we're going back to the casino," Mr. Mack announced. "This will be the last experiment, on a different table. So far, it's working perfectly."

"That's terrific, Dad," Annie said sincerely, but impatient to discover what had happened to Alex. "I'm sure you'll win lots of money. Now, Ray, we'd better head off before Alex decides to start without us." She grabbed his arm and hurried him away. As soon as they were out of earshot of their parents, she asked: "Where's Alex?"

"We saw Big Al," Ray explained. "And Alex left to trail him."

"And you just *let* her?" Annie cried. "Ray, the guy's a thug!"

"I didn't have much choice," Ray said glumly. "I had to keep our folks from finding out what was going on. But now we can go after her—if we know where to go."

"I've discovered where he's staying," Annie answered. "He's bound to head back there. If he's still got the book, maybe we can get it back. At any rate, I hope we're in time to help Alex out."

Lars was getting very confused with Annie's running around. She hadn't gone straight to the hotel, after all, for the meeting. Instead, she'd met up with the Macks again, and now that next-door neighbor of theirs was going with her. Then Lars grinned. She was pulling another trick, just in case she was being followed. She must have given the notebook to Ray and acted as a decoy herself for a while. And *now* they were heading for that room she'd indicated on the computer.

Which meant it was time for him to get there first.

Liseta was feeling very nervous now. She'd had to return to Big Al and inform him that the girl Thomas had seen with the book wasn't in the ladies' room after all. The news hadn't made Big Al happy.

"But I saw her go in, boss!" Thomas protested. "She's *got* to be in there."

"She isn't," Liseta insisted. Thomas had described a blond teenager, which sounded to her like Annie's kid sister. How Alex could possibly have managed to get the book, she couldn't say. But she didn't intend to tell Al that the girl might be one of the Macks. Al had a terrible temper, and there was no telling what he might do in his attempts to get the girl back.

Al glared at her suspiciously. "Are you sure you're not covering for her?" he growled. "You seem to be getting awfully soft about this caper."

"I'm telling you the truth," Liseta insisted. "The only person in there is a dark-haired woman in her twenties." The door opened, and the woman walked out. "And that's her. There's nobody else in there. Send Thomas in if you don't believe me."

Al thought for a second, and then nodded. Thomas blushed—the first time he'd shown any kind of emotion that Liseta had ever seen—but he went inside. He emerged a moment later, still red, and puzzled.

"She's right, boss. The place is empty."

"This is screwy," Al decided. "It's like we're haunted or something. Bathtubs that turn themselves on. A girl who vanishes. And that idiot detective." He turned to Thomas. "Did Jerry get him?"

Thomas shook his head. "He managed to get away too, boss."

"I'm surrounded by idiots!" Al yelled, throwing up his hands in disgust. "I'll have to wipe your noses for you next!" He thought for a minute, and Liseta started to get worried again. "Okay, whoever took that book will try to get it back to the Macks, obviously. Liseta, you and I will go and meet the family in the casino again. Thomas, you follow us, and keep your eyes peeled for that girl. If she turns up, grab her. And have Jerry find that detective. I want him out of the way, too!"

"Okay, boss." Thomas hurried away.

Liseta frowned, but kept quiet. It was bad enough to have stolen the book from Annie in the first place. She felt really guilty about taking advantage of the young girl like that. But now Al seemed to have declared war on the Mack family. "What are you going to do?" she asked him.

He gave her a dark look. "I'm running out of patience. That Mack guy is our ticket to a fortune. If we don't get that book back soon, then I'm going to have to put the snatch on Mack and get it from him by more direct means."

Liseta had a sinking feeling in her stomach. Al was intending to kidnap Annie's father!

Alex didn't know how far she'd gone, or in what direction. She'd just slid with the flow of the pipe. She was used to the piping in her family home by now, but this was definitely strange territory. Side pipes turned off at any number of points, but she didn't know which way to go. She was lost in the plumbing of Las Vegas!

And she could feel the strain of remaining in her liquid form. She'd done too much of it already today, and she knew she'd have to return to her human shape any minute now. And she couldn't do that in this narrow piping.

So she had no choice. She took the next side pipe, and shot down it as fast as she could. This had better lead somewhere out of the system, or she was going to be in serious trouble! More pipes led off this one, and she chose one at random to go down. The pipes were getting narrower all the time, which suggested that they had to lead somewhere soon.

And then she saw light ahead of her—dim, but real. An exit! And just in time. She could feel the strain in her body from holding this state for too long. Once she was out of here, she'd have to stay in her human form for hours before she could morph again. Still, with luck that shouldn't be any problem. She had to have managed to give Al and his men the slip now. She didn't have a clue as to where in Vegas she was, so there was no way that he could possibly predict where she'd be. She was bound to be safe.

Then she came to a small grating, and slipped up through it. She found herself on a concrete floor, surrounded by plants of some kind. There was nobody in sight. With a sigh of relief, Alex morphed back to a human being.

She was sitting in some kind of jungle, but the look of things puzzled her. This had to be one of the theme parks, she supposed; maybe the MGM? There was an odd smell, too, that she couldn't quite place. Puzzled, she decided to stand up and get a good look around.

As Alex did so, she froze in fear. She suddenly knew exactly where she had ended up.

Staring at her from about ten feet away was a white tiger. And there were the sounds of others beyond that one.

Alex almost fainted with fear. She'd emerged inside the white tiger habitat, and the tigers knew she was there.

CHAPTER 8

Alex's throat had gone dry, and her knees were on the verge of giving way as she stared back at the white tiger facing her. Its mouth was open, and she could see the saliva dripping from the very large fangs. Twin blue eyes glared at her in anger. She realized that it viewed her as an intruder in his territory, and it wasn't going to stand for that.

She was seconds away from being torn to pieces.

She couldn't simply morph to escape, because her body was far too tired for that. It needed to rest and recuperate before she could liquefy again. Trying to fight back her feelings of panic and impending death, Alex concentrated her mind as she stared hard at the tiger.

Its tail lashed, and she could see the muscles in its body tense as it prepared to leap at her. She couldn't possibly get out of the way in time; it was much bigger and faster than she was. So she had to stop it.

Easy to say! But she reached out with her telekinetic powers. The only way to stop it from leaping at her was to make certain it couldn't leap at all. It was a strain affecting anything the size and weight of the tiger, but Alex had no other option. She used her powers to form a force field around it to contain it.

The tiger gave a startled yelp as it realized it couldn't leap at her. It flailed about in confusion, striving to break through the invisible barrier, but she wasn't about to let that happen! Watching the startled tiger carefully, she edged back from where she had been standing.

She'd come up through the drain in the floor near the rear of the tiger enclosure. Somewhere behind her had to be the door the keepers used to come into the cage. If she could find that, she could—hopefully!—get out. She didn't dare look over her shoulder. There were other tigers out in the enclosure, and they were bound to have scented her by now. If they came to investigate, she'd be in even more trouble. Holding one tiger captive like this was straining her powers already. She'd never manage to imprison any more.

Then her back came in contact with the rear wall, and she felt a sense of relief. She slowly moved along the wall, her hand held out, feeling for wherever the door might be.

There was a low growl, and a second tiger emerged from the shrubs to stare at the first one. The first tiger gave a whimper of fear, and tried to regain its freedom, slamming hard against the invisible barrier surrounding it. The second tiger gave a *whuff* of surprise, and then it saw Alex.

Now she was in for it! She'd never be able to stop the second tiger as well!

Instead, she did the only thing she could think of: she flung the first tiger at the second with every ounce of force she could muster. Both animals went into a squalling bundle, shocked by what had happened. Alex glanced around and saw the door, just a couple of feet away. No longer holding up a heavy tiger, she walked quickly to the door, and probed it with her powers. Naturally, it was locked.

Quickly, she sent a zap into the mechanism to loosen the lock. She had to split her attention between it and the two tigers. The big cats were clambering back to their feet, puzzled but angry. Both of them started moving toward her, a low growling in their throats indicating their mood. Feeling sick, Alex stopped work on the lock for a second. She'd never be able to lift both of them, so instead she used her zap. One blast of electricity slammed into the first tiger's nose, and another into the second.

Both yowled and jumped back, clearly shaken by this new assault. They pawed at their noses in irritation, and eyed Alex with fresh respect— and anger. They weren't about to give up, but they would be more cautious. Slowly, they started forward again.

Frantic now, Alex used her powers on the lock again, and this time she heard a *click* as the lock sprang open. She shoved the door and stumbled through it. She swung it closed behind her as the two tigers charged it. The lock clicked back into place just as the first tiger launched himself at the door. Alex yelped and ducked instinctively as the tiger slammed into the door. It shook from the impact but held firm.

Alex felt like melting into a pool of goo right now—not using her powers, just from shock and relief. Her whole body was trembling, and she knew how serious the situation had been. She was simply lucky that she'd been able to rattle the tigers by using her powers. She leaned against the wall, taking deep breaths to steady her pounding heart and churning stomach. Much as she had enjoyed seeing the tigers on-stage the previous night, *this* had been way too close a view to make her happy!

She'd just rest for a couple of minutes to get her breath and her poise back, Alex decided. Then she'd sneak out of the security area using her powers. At least she now knew that she was in the Mirage Hotel. Once she was out of here, she could go and find Annie and Ray and figure out what they'd do next.

Lars had a feeling of tremendous satisfaction as he hurried down the corridor to the four-teenth-floor room where Annie was going to make contact with the man from Keystone Petro-chemicals. The Macks thought they'd outsmarted everyone, but nobody could outthink Lars Frederickson. He'd make sure that he was ready for them!

Reaching the right door, he rapped on it loudly. "Room service!" he called. Then he waited. As he'd hoped, there was no response from inside. He was definitely in plenty of time to observe the meeting and get all the proof he needed. He had a camera in his pocket to record the incriminating data, and a tape recorder. He took out his computer probe, and started to work on the lock. All he needed was a few seconds, and he'd be able to slip inside and find somewhere to hide and then—

—he felt a large hand clamp onto his shoulder, and whirled around, astonished. The door across the hall was open, and a tall, wiry man had emerged to grab him. The man smiled nastily. "Lost your key, have you?" he asked, dragging Lars away from the door.

"Er, yes, that's right," Lars said quickly, too startled to think straight.

"A likely story," the man said with a snort. "That's not your room, and this little device looks like a burglary tool to me." He gave another wide grin. "I'm the house detective, sir, and I'd like you to come with me. We take breaking and entering very seriously in this hotel."

"No, wait," Lars protested. "You don't understand!"

"Oh, I understand all right, sir," the detective answered. "We've had reports of suspicious goings-on on this floor, and I've been waiting for you. But if you need a sympathetic ear, I'm sure the local police would just *love* to hear your story!" He dragged the protesting Lars off toward the elevators.

Annie and Ray reached the hotel where Big Al Drury had his room and then headed for the elevators. As they did so, however, they heard a loud *psst!* from behind a potted palm. Puzzled, Annie stopped and peered through the thick foliage. "Sam Ace!" she exclaimed.

"Ssh!" Sam begged her. "Come here, quick."

Annie sighed. "We don't have time for games, Sam."

"This isn't a game," he assured her. "Please!"

Annie glanced at Ray, who shrugged. Then they both hurried around the palm. "What is it?" she asked.

"Drury's got his men out looking for me," Sam explained. "He caught me snooping on his balcony. I was lucky to get this far, but there's one of his men watching the door. I need help to get out of here."

"And I need help to get in here," Annie told him. "I think my sister's up in his room. He took something from us that she's trying to get back."

Sam's eyes widened. "A notebook?" he asked.

"That's right." Annie didn't like telling him anything, because he might get a little too curious as to what was in it, but he obviously knew something about it.

"Then it's not there," Sam told her. "Big Al and his men are hunting for it right now. Somehow, it just vanished from his room."

Annie couldn't resist a grin. That *had* to be Alex's doing! So she already had the book back. "Well, that's a relief," she said.

"Right," agreed Ray. "So I guess we don't need to go up to his room and try to rescue Alex."

"I wouldn't be so sure of that," Sam told them, and Annie felt ice chill her heart. "Al's furious, and he's got all of his men out now. He must really want whatever's in that book very badly.

If your sister has it, then she's likely to be in serious trouble."

Annie was shocked, and worried for Alex. "Then we can't stand here talking with you," she said firmly. "We'd better find Alex." She started to leave, but he grabbed hold of her arm.

"You'll do better with my help," Sam assured her. "The three of us stand a better chance of stopping him."

"He's got a point there," Ray conceded.

Annie weighed up the time lost in helping Sam against the addition of an extra person to search and help out. She decided a short delay would be worth it. "Okay," she said reluctantly. "What do you want us to do?"

"There's a store over there," he replied. "I need a coat, hat, and dark glasses. Then, once I'm disguised, we can slip past Jerry over there and get after your sister." He handed her several bills. "Please!"

"All right," she agreed. "Just wait here a minute. Ray, you stay with him. I'll be faster on my own." She slipped back into the lobby again and hurried to the shop. As she made her purchases, she couldn't help being worried sick about her sister. It looked as though Alex had the book back and had made her getaway, but Big Al clearly wasn't giving up. The lure of the millions that might be made using her father's formula clearly had intoxicated the crook. She wondered just how far he'd dare to go to get what he wanted. And she didn't dare tell the police or anyone about all of this, because they would want to get hold of the notebook for evidence. And that would mean the end of Alex's freedom.

She hurried back to the detective with his fresh disguise. She'd bought a large coat and a floppy hat, along with mirrored sunglasses. After putting them on, Sam looked very different. Annie wasn't sure that the disguise would work, so she'd added a couple of touches of her own— Mylar balloons declaring that she loved Las Vegas.

"Stay with us," she told Sam, handing one balloon to Ray.

"What's with the kids' stuff?" he asked her.

"Ray and I will float the balloons in front of the thug's face," Annie explained. "That, coupled with your disguise, should get us past him."

"It's that tall, beefy-looking guy over by the door," Sam pointed out to her. Annie examined the man, and saw that he was indeed the body-builder type.

"Ouch," she muttered. "I wouldn't want to get on his bad side. Right, come on. Talk all the way. If they're looking for you as you, they'll expect you to be on your own, not part of a group."

"That makes sense," Sam agreed. "Annie, you're quite a smart kid. Have you ever considered taking up detective work?"

"In a manner of speaking," she answered with a grin. "I'm hoping to become a research scientist when I graduate." They were getting close to Jerry, who was scanning the crowd in the lobby. Annie couldn't help feeling apprehensive. If he saw through Sam's disguise . . . Annie held the balloon at just the right height to block Jerry's direct view of Sam, and Ray had his on the far side of Sam. It was like protective camouflage on an animal, blurring Sam's profile. It *should* work. . . .

She almost held her breath as they passed right by Jerry. Ray, somehow, was babbling on about wanting to go on one of the roller coaster rides, and how much he loved it when they defied gravity. "I hate that stuff," she said. "I want to see the horses. They're *cute*." She put as much whine into her voice as she could.

Jerry didn't even bother looking at them. As she'd suspected, he was looking for a lone man trying to get out, not a family group. Still, she could almost feel his eyes on her back as they headed out of the hotel and into the street.

"Made it," Ray gasped. "Wow, was I ever nervous there."

"You both did fine," Sam assured them. "Now, where will Alex have gone if she's got the book back?"

"To the casino," Annie decided. "She'll expect us to be there waiting for her." She handed her balloon to a surprised passing child. "Free gift," she told the young girl. Ray got rid of his the same way. "Let's get moving, guys!"

Together, they hurried down the Strip.

Barbara Mack was having a marvelous time. Everyone in the room seemed to be watching George as he placed his next bet. He had a huge pile of chips in front of him now. She had no real idea how much he had actually won, but it was obviously a great deal of money. He calculated the figures in his head and then announced: "Six."

The croupier nodded, and moved his bet to number 6. Mr. Alvarado was almost bouncing up and down with excitement. "This is incredible, George, just incredible."

"No, no," Mr. Mack replied, distracted. "It's merely an application of scientific theory. A test. It seems to be working very well, though. This is the third wheel, and they've all behaved exactly according to theory, which is most encouraging."

"And it's exciting, too," Mrs. Mack added. She was enjoying having a crowd of people gathered around watching her husband at work. She was so proud of him.

The roulette wheel was started up, and the ball spun. Everyone watched as the ball flew around, and then the air was incredibly thick with tension as the wheel slowed and the ball started to drop into a groove.

"Number six," the croupier announced, and there was a wild cheer from all around. Mr. Mack looked rather bemused by this, and then smiled at his wife.

"I think that's enough, don't you?" he suggested. "My theory's been proven by now, I think."

"I agree," Mrs. Mack replied. She leaned forward and took a hundred dollars' worth of chips off the nearest of his piles.

"One last bet," her husband said. "Number eight." The croupier placed the bet, and then everyone held their breath as the wheel started up again.

The tension was incredible. Mr. Alvarado stared at the ball, as if willing it into place. Nobody seemed to be breathing, even, as the ball slowly settled into place. . . .

"Number twenty-three," the operator announced, and there was a chorus of groans and commiserations.

"I don't believe it!" Mr. Alvarado explained. "You *lost!*"

Mr. and Mrs. Mack were the only ones who didn't seem to be disturbed by this. "Of course we lost," Mr. Mack said, puzzled. "I made sure we would."

For a moment, Mr. Alvarado was speechless. Then he croaked: "But . . . but *why?*"

"Because it would have been ethically wrong to win money using my formula," Mr. Mack replied. "It would have given me an unfair advantage. I was only doing this as a scientific experiment, as I told you when we started. I had no intentions of ever keeping the money."

His wife gave him a peck on the cheek. "I am so proud of you, George," she said. "Your formula works perfectly."

Mr. Alvarado stared at the chips the cashier was raking in, and shook his head sadly. "I can't believe you *deliberately* gave back over twenty-five thousand dollars! Didn't you want to keep it?"

Mr. Mack patted him kindly on the arm. "It would have been like stealing," he explained. "I feel much better giving it back."

"Well, *I* don't," Mr. Alvarado answered. Then he hit himself on the forehead. "I was so busy watching you play, I didn't even place any bets of my own! I haven't won a thing, either!"

"It's better that way," Mrs. Mack told him. "And you haven't lost anything, either." She held up the chips. "And here's our original hundred dollars back again. Everything worked out fine."

"I suppose," Mr. Alvarado said, looking longingly at the chips. Then he smiled. "So, how about we get tickets to see Tony Bennett now?"

Alex rushed breathlessly into the casino lobby, clutching Annie's notebook. There she paused to recover, while looking around. There was no sign of either Ray or Annie. Presumably the adults were still in the casino, but she couldn't go in there to check. Now what? The only thing she could think of was to check in with Annie at their hotel room, in case she was still there, so she went to one of the public phones.

She dialed the hotel number, and then asked for their room. The operator tried, but informed Alex that there was no reply. Alex thanked her and hung up. So Annie wasn't there, either. Now what?

As she considered her options, she saw three new arrivals in the lobby that she did recognize—and didn't want to be seen by. Big Al, Thomas, and Liseta walked in through the main entrance. Alex ducked back into the telephone alcove, and watched. Al Drury looked furious, and she knew that he had to be up to something.

*   *   *

Liseta was almost frantic now. She'd tried talking Big Al out of his plan to kidnap the Macks, with absolutely no success. He was obsessed with the desire to get rich, and he saw George Mack as his key to this. Liseta had been forced to shut up finally, as he'd glowered at her and accused her of trying to betray him. But she still didn't like his plans.

Now they were in the casino lobby, and Al gestured to Thomas. "Check that they're still in there," he ordered. "If they are, we'll lure them out by pretending their daughter is sick. I'll have Jerry bring the car to the front of the casino. Once we've got them in that, we'll take them out to the desert until they agree to cooperate." He fingered the walkie-talkie in his pocket and then strode over to the telephone alcove to place the call.

As he did so, Liseta had a quick glimpse of a familiar face ducking back out of sight. It was Alex Mack! She had to be hiding in there—and Al was going to stumble across her any second!

CHAPTER 9

Alex saw with horror that Big Al was heading directly toward her. There was nowhere to hide in here, and she still wasn't able to morph—even if she'd dared to try it in this busy lobby. Once he saw her, he was bound to try to get the book back again. And Alex couldn't call for help because she didn't want to have to explain what was in the notebook to anyone in authority.

There was only one thing she could think of doing. As Al passed one of the potted palms, Alex used all of her mental strength to push at it. With a creak, the palm swayed, and then collapsed, just as Al was next to it. He gave a startled yelp as the plant fell down on top of him. While he was struggling to free himself from its leafy embrace, Alex ducked out of the alcove and dashed for cover behind another of the plants.

She'd avoided being discovered, but how long could she keep this up? People would think that the palm toppling over was an accident, but she could hardly expect them to believe it if she had to produce one "accident" after another to stop him.

Annie dashed through the doors of the casino to see a scene of confusion. People were milling around a man on the floor, who seemed to have been attacked by one of the ever-present potted palms. When Annie recognized the man as Big Al, she realized that this meant only one thing. "Alex is already here," she told Ray. "We've got to find her and help her."

"How do you know that?" asked Sam, puzzled.

"It's a trade secret," Annie answered. As she scanned the lobby, she suddenly saw Liseta Lopez heading directly toward her. "Uh-oh. Trouble. We'd better split."

"Annie, wait!" Liseta called. "Please!"

Annie hesitated. Liseta had stolen the book from her after pretending to be her friend. She couldn't trust the young woman. And yet she did seem to be very sincere and worried. After a moment of indecision, Annie waited.

"Your father is in serious trouble," Liseta said, urgently gripping Annie's arm. "Big Al has decided that he will kidnap him and get the secret of his system that way."

"Why should I believe you?" Annie asked bitterly. "You've lied to me once already by pretending you were my friend and then stealing from me."

There were tears in the corners of Liseta's eyes. "I had no choice," she said, in almost a whisper. "Big Al forced me to do it. But he cannot force me to help hurt your family any further."

Sam stepped forward, and removed his sunglasses. "Miss Lopez," he said, "I don't get it. Why are you turning on him now, since you work for him?"

Liseta's eyes widened. "You're the detective after him!" she exclaimed.

"If you want us to believe you," Annie said, "then you've got to give us a reason to do so. Tell us why you're helping us."

"Because," said a familiar voice, "Big Al's forcing her to work for him."

Annie gave a laugh of delight. "Alex! You're okay!"

Alex nodded, and handed her sister the notebook. "You'd better keep this safe." Then she explained what she'd overheard at the hotel.

"It's true," Liseta admitted, bowing her head in shame. "Most of what I told you earlier is true, Annie. I am from Guatemala, and I do support my family there. Big Al forced me to help him in his scams because he said he would harm my family if I didn't. I discovered later that he was lying about this, and he can't hurt them. But now he promises that if he's ever arrested, he'll make sure that I go to jail and then get deported. And if that happens, there will be no one who will look after my family. My brothers and sisters will starve. I couldn't let that happen, so I had to stay and work for Big Al."

Annie wondered if this was just another story that Liseta had made up. But then she saw the young woman's face, and her eyes brimming with tears. If it *was* a lie, Liseta had to be the best actress she'd ever seen. She was certain that this time Liseta was telling the truth. And she was clearly not the only person who believed her.

Sam's face had a very angry expression on it. "That's another lie, Liseta," he told her. "If you agree to turn state's evidence against Al Drury, I'll put in a good word for you with the district attorney. You'll be let off without being prosecuted, I promise you. And you won't get deported, either."

Liseta looked doubtful, and then hopeful. "You can arrange this?" she asked, amazed.

"I promise you, I can," Sam assured her.

Annie was proud of him. He'd seemed like such an idiot earlier, but now he was actually coming through for Liseta. She realized that his problem was a lack of confidence in himself. He really hadn't been sure that he could nail Al Drury. And all his schemes seemed to have gone wrong, which lowered his self-confidence even further. Now, however, he had a star witness on his side, and the end of his case was in sight.

Except for the major problem that Big Al was going to try and kidnap her parents!

Barbara Mack felt very happy about the way things had turned out. George had tested and

proven his new formula, and she'd had a lot of
fun watching him winning at roulette. It had
been a little painful seeing him give the money
back, but she knew that he was right. Keeping
money that he'd effectively cheated to win
would have been wrong.

Even if they *could* have used twenty-five thousand dollars!

Still, it was nice to have simply had it for a
while, and she knew that having a clear con-
science was more important than having lots of
money in the bank. Mr. Alvarado was still a little
upset about it, though.

"Come on, George," he begged, as they
headed for the lobby. "Just give me a couple of
tips, so I can win a little money, huh?"

"I'm sorry," Mr. Mack answered. "It just
wouldn't be right." He clapped his friend on the
back. "But we can still have fun in Vegas without a million dollars, can't we?"

"We could have more fun *with* a million dollars," muttered Mr. Alvarado. He seemed to
have realized that he wasn't going to get it,
though, and smiled ruefully. "I guess you're
right, George. Money isn't everything." His eyes
lit up. "But music is. . . . Tony Bennett tonight,

and then maybe one of the Elvis imperson-
ators? Huh?"

Mrs. Mack pointed at the doorway. "Here's
that man you were talking to earlier, George. Mr.
Drury, wasn't it? I wonder what he wants."

Alex saw that Big Al had managed to get back
to his feet and he'd brushed off all offers of help.
After making his call, he hurried through the
doors into the casino. "We've got to stop him!"
she exclaimed.

"This is my job," Sam said firmly. He threw
off his hat and dashed after Big Al and Thomas.

Alex winced. Sam was being very brave, but
also more than a little foolish. Thomas could
snap him in half without working up a sweat.
She had to do something to help him, and stop
him from getting badly beaten up.

The two crooks were passing by the slot ma-
chines, and Alex had the perfect solution. Using
her telekinetic powers, she clicked the tumblers
of the closest spare machine over to the jackpot
combination.

There was a blare of music, and a flash of
lights, and then coins started to gush out of the
machine, and cascaded onto the floor. Alex had

been hoping just to distract the two men, but her plan worked better than she'd hoped. Thomas gave a strangled cry as he stepped on a wave of the coins, and his feet flew out from under him.

"Drury!" Sam yelled, as he rushed up. Big Al spun around, confused, and then saw who was behind him.

"Why, you . . ." he began, but didn't have the chance to say anything else. Arms flailing wildly, he stepped onto the shower of coins, and lost his footing, too. He slammed heavily into Thomas, who was struggling to get to his feet, and the two men went down in a heap.

Security guards started running across the room toward the struggle. Alex, Annie, Liseta, and Ray all hurried into the casino to join the Macks and Mr. Alvarado, who were watching everything with very puzzled expressions.

"Do any of you know what's going on here?" Mrs. Mack asked.

"It's a long story," Alex replied. "Maybe we could all have dinner together with one of the greatest private eyes in the world?" She gestured at Sam, who was explaining everything to the chief security guard. Several of his men were helping Big Al and Thomas to their feet—and keeping their beefy fists on the villains' arms.

"This," Mr. Mack said, looking at the confusion, "I have got to hear."

Alex really enjoyed their dinner at Mizumo's. It was one of those Japanese restaurants where the chef cooks the food for you right on the table. Their chef had shown a dizzying dexterity with his ginsu knives, chopping, slicing, and moving vegetables, shrimps, and steaks about. He'd tossed peas at Annie, chopped off the tails of shrimps and thrown them in the air, catching them in his hat, and generally behaved like a maniac, having them all laughing.

In between the food, everyone had explained as much of the story as they could. Sam and Liseta had joined the Macks and Alvarados, and Sam had detailed most of the case, with some comments from Annie. Alex had wisely kept quiet. Somehow she didn't think her parents would have liked to have heard about her breaking into a crook's room or being trapped in a cage full of white tigers. . . .

"Well," Mr. Mack said in amazement, "I really had no idea that any of this was going on at all.

Mr. Ace, you really *are* a wonderful detective. Thank you for looking after my daughters."

"I'm glad I could help," Sam replied. "Actually, I have the strangest feeling that someone was looking after me. I almost fell off Drury's balcony, and something invisible seemed to grab me and help me back. And that shower of coins that stopped Big Al came from a machine nobody was even playing." Alex winced, wondering if he suspected something, but he went on: "I feel like I've got a guardian angel watching over me. And in my business, that's really kind of useful."

"As long as you don't rely on it," Alex put in quickly, hoping Sam wasn't about to start taking crazy risks when she wasn't around to help him out.

"No way," he agreed. "I've learned my lesson. From now on, I'm going to be a lot more careful. No more risking my neck if I can avoid it."

"That's good news," Annie said with a smile for Alex. She turned to Liseta. "And how did things go for you?"

Liseta gave a wide smile. "Wonderfully. Sam kept his word, and I had a long talk with the district attorney. I am to be given immunity from prosecution, in return for my testimony against

Big Al, Thomas, and Jerry. They will be going to jail for a long time. And I will not be deported." She smiled at Sam. "And Sam has asked me to come and work for him as his assistant, so I can earn an honest living. This way, I can continue to support my family."

Sam blushed. "Well, since the word's gotten out that I've managed to nail Big Al, I've suddenly been offered a lot of jobs. I need the help."

Alex couldn't help smiling. Despite her initial distrust of Liseta, the young woman had turned out to be very pleasant. She'd only worked for Big Al because she'd been scared and blackmailed into it. When it counted, she'd helped out the Macks and given Sam his big break. Alex couldn't help feeling good about how everything had turned out. They still had two more days of vacation left, which was plenty of time to see everything that she wanted to. And, best of all, there had been absolutely no problems with Danielle Atron for once. Despite her worries, Paradise Valley Chemical had done nothing here in Vegas at all.

Danielle answered the telephone with ice in her voice. "Lars," she purred, like a tiger. "What is it that you want?"

"Uh, Ms. Atron, I don't quite know how to tell you this," he said. She could hear the embarrassment and irritation in his voice.

"You'd better do it directly, Lars," she answered. "Or else I'm hanging up on you."

"I need you to post bail for me, Ms. Atron."

"What?" Danielle couldn't believe what she was hearing. "Lars, what *have* you done?"

She could almost hear him wincing. "The Las Vegas police have arrested me for attempted breaking and entering," he explained. He sounded more incensed than contrite. "I was trying to beat Mack to the rendezvous he'd planned to sell his formula, and they thought I was a burglar."

Danielle had to count to ten to avoid either screaming or sending her blood pressure through the ceiling. "Lars," she finally said. "You're a fool. George Mack called me an hour ago to tell me that his vacation in Las Vegas had so relaxed him that he'd been able to finish work on his formula. And then he faxed it to me."

"He did . . . what?" Lars asked weakly.

"So," Danielle plowed on, "your paranoid fantasies about his selling secrets to Keystone Petrochemical have proven to be completely unfounded. As I always knew, Mack is a loyal and dedicated worker. And he hasn't managed to get himself into any trouble whatsoever—unlike you." She forced herself to calm down again. "So, as far as I'm concerned, you can stay in jail until I feel like paying to get you back." She slammed down the phone, and then took a deep breath to compose herself again.

Lars was such a fool sometimes. But he was also a useful tool. She'd let him rot in jail for a day or so, and then bail him out. He'd be so pathetically grateful that he'd do anything for her that she asked after that. And she had some delightful new ideas she wanted to try out. Danielle smiled, and glanced down at the formula George Mack had faxed her. She didn't understand it—she was a businesswoman, after all, not a scientist—but if it did what Mack claimed, then it would be highly useful.

It had been a good day for her, after all.

About the Author

JOHN PEEL was born in Nottingham, England—
home of Robin Hood. He moved to the United
States in 1981 to get married and now lives on
Long Island with his wife, Nan, their wirehaired
fox terrier, Dashiell, and their feline terror,
Amika. He has written more than seventy books,
including novels based on the top British science
fiction TV series *Doctor Who*, and the top Ameri-
can science fiction TV series *Star Trek*. He has
written several supernatural thrillers for young
adults that are published by Archway Paperbacks—*Talons*, *Shattered*, *Poison*, and *Maniac*. *Star
Trek: Deep Space Nine: Prisoners of Peace* and *Field
Trip* are available from Minstrel Books.

John has written several Nickelodeon titles for the
Are You Afraid of the Dark?, *The Secret World of Alex
Mack*, and *The Mystery Files of Shelby Woo* series.

Sometimes, it takes a kid to solve a good crime....

Original stories based on the hit Nickelodeon show!

#1 A Slash in the Night
by Alan Goodman

#2 Takeout Stakeout
By Diana G. Gallagher

#3 Hot Rock
by John Peel

#4 Rock 'n' Roll Robbery
by Lydia C. Marano and David Cody Weiss

To find out more about *The Mystery Files of Shelby Woo* or any other Nickelodeon show, visit Nickelodeon Online on America Online (Keyword: NICK) or send e-mail (NickMailDD@aol.com).

 A MINSTREL® BOOK

Published by Pocket Books

1338-03

What's it like to be a Witch?

Sabrina ☆
The Teenage
Witch™

"I'm 16, I'm a Witch,
and I still have to go to school?"

◆◆◆◆◆◆◆◆

From Archway Paperbacks
Published by Pocket Books

1346-01

Have you ever wished for the complete guide to surviving your teenage years? At long last, here's your owner's manual—a book of instructions and insights into exactly how YOU operate.

LET'S TALK ABOUT ME!

A Girl's Personal, Private, and Portable
Instruction Book for life

Learn what makes boys so weird
Discover the hidden meanings in your doodles
Uncover the person you want to be
Get to know yourself better than anyone else on Earth
Laugh a little
Think a little
Grow a little

TOP-SECRET QUIZZES, COOL ACTIVITIES, AND MUCH, MUCH MORE

Being a teenage girl
has never been so much fun!

**From the creators of
the bestselling CD-ROM!**

An Archway Paperback
Published by Pocket Books

1384-01

Are You Afraid of the Dark?®

#1 THE TALE OF THE SINISTER STATUES 52545-X/$3.99

#2 THE TALE OF CUTTER'S TREASURE 52729-0/$3.99

#3 THE TALE OF THE RESTLESS HOUSE 52547-6/$3.99

#4 THE TALE OF THE NIGHTLY NEIGHBORS 53445-9/$3.99

#5 THE TALE OF THE SECRET MIRROR 53671-0/$3.99

#6 THE TALE OF THE PHANTOM SCHOOL BUS 53672-9/$3.99

#7 THE TALE OF THE GHOST RIDERS 56252-5/$3.99

#8 THE TALE OF THE DEADLY DIARY 53673-7/$3.99

#9 THE TALE OF THE VIRTUAL NIGHTMARE 00080-2/$3.99

#10 THE TALE OF THE CURIOUS CAT 00081-0/$3.99

#11 THE TALE OF THE ZERO HERO 00357-7/$3.99

#12 THE TALE OF THE SHIMMERING SHELL 00392-5/$3.99

#13 THE TALE OF THE THREE WISHES 00358-5/$3.99

#14 THE TALE OF THE CAMPFIRE VAMPIRES 00908-7/$3.99

#15 THE TALE OF THE BAD-TEMPERED GHOST 01429-3/$3.99

#16 TALE OF THE SOUVENIR SHOP 00909-5/$3.99

#17 THE TALE OF THE GHOST CRUISE 01439-0/$3.99

A MINSTREL® BOOK

Simon & Schuster Mail Order Dept. BWB
200 Old Tappan Rd., Old Tappan, N.J. 07675

Please send me the books I have checked above. I am enclosing $_____ (please add $0.75 to cover the postage and handling for each order. Please add appropriate sales tax). Send check or money order--no cash or C.O.D.'s please. Allow up to six weeks for delivery. For purchase over $10.00 you may use VISA: card number, expiration date and customer signature must be included.

Name _____

Address _____

City _____ State/Zip _____

VISA Card # _____ Exp.Date _____

Signature _____

1053-16